"Charley,"  voice oozi

Jane touched ___ ___ ___ ___ ___ ___ swallowed, trying desperately to keep his cool. To not let her see that her touch had sent a jolt through him.

"You're all I've thought about for months. In every dream. In every shower. It's been you. Just...you."

It was time to leave. She was his secretary—she had temporary amnesia. She thought they were a couple. Time to run as fast as he could in any direction. But her fingers held him captive.

Her mouth, her moist scarlet lips, curved once more into the smile of a temptress. Those eyes...

Dammit. He grabbed her arms with his hands, pulling her close to his now stirring body. His mouth covered hers and he stole her very breath.

Crazy. He was insane. This situation was insane.

But a loaded pistol couldn't have stopped him. Hell, a whole army couldn't have stopped him from making love to his "fiancée."

Dear Reader,

The idea for *Ms. Taken* kind of bonked me over the head, much like the little incident that happens to Jane in the story. I was minding my own business and I was "struck" with the notion that sometimes we hide our real, vibrant, charming inner selves because we think we should. That people wouldn't understand.

And then I thought—so what? Who cares what other people think? Being true to ourselves...ah, that's something worth fighting for. Worth *living* for.

Thus Jane was born, filled with doubts, hiding behind a wall of propriety, living the life she was supposed to. Her inner world, however, was filled with lust and love and romance and a particularly yummy boss named Charles.

That is until the fateful day when she was minding her own business and— Oops. I don't want to spoil the rest. Just let me say that working on THE PERSONAL TOUCH! miniseries was a joy from beginning to end. I hope you see a little of yourself in Jane, and that it won't take a conk on the head to show you how wonderful you are.

I love to hear from readers. You can contact me at www.joleigh.com.

Best wishes,

Jo Leigh

Books by Jo Leigh

HARLEQUIN TEMPTATION
699—SINGLE SHERIFF SEEKS
727—TANGLED SHEETS
756—HOT AND BOTHERED

MS. TAKEN
Jo Leigh

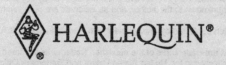

HARLEQUIN®

TORONTO • NEW YORK • LONDON
AMSTERDAM • PARIS • SYDNEY • HAMBURG
STOCKHOLM • ATHENS • TOKYO • MILAN • MADRID
PRAGUE • WARSAW • BUDAPEST • AUCKLAND

To Debbi and Peter,
for making me (and the kitties)
part of the family.

ISBN 0-373-25909-3

MS. TAKEN

Copyright © 2000 by Jolie Kramer.

All rights reserved. Except for use in any review, the reproduction or
utilization of this work in whole or in part in any form by any electronic,
mechanical or other means, now known or hereafter invented, including
xerography, photocopying and recording, or in any information storage
or retrieval system, is forbidden without the written permission of the
publisher, Harlequin Enterprises Limited, 225 Duncan Mill Road,
Don Mills, Ontario, Canada M3B 3K9.

All characters in this book have no existence outside the imagination of
the author and have no relation whatsoever to anyone bearing the same
name or names. They are not even distantly inspired by any individual
known or unknown to the author, and all incidents are pure invention.

This edition published by arrangement with Harlequin Books S.A.

® and TM are trademarks of the publisher. Trademarks indicated with
® are registered in the United States Patent and Trademark Office, the
Canadian Trade Marks Office and in other countries.

Visit us at www.eHarlequin.com

Printed in U.S.A.

1

ONE ORANGE. Five Triscuits. Three baby carrots. One ounce Jarlsberg cheese, cubed. Two Oreo cookies.

Jane Dobson smiled at the perfection that was her lunch. The napkin, a new color for her, blue, had unfolded on her desk in a nice, neat square to reveal each item of food just as she'd packed it this morning. No crumbs. Not a one. That Hello Kitty lunch pail was really doing the job.

Peeling the orange came next, which wasn't easy because her nails were so short. She tried not to bite them, honestly. But it was hard to catch herself in the act. Mostly, she'd just notice her fingers as she typed, and the nails would be bitten to the quick.

Oh, well. It's not as if she was a hand model or anything. Besides, short nails made her really fast on the computer. She'd clocked herself at nearly one hundred words-per only last week. Four words more than a month ago.

She ended up biting the orange peel, getting a squirt of that really sour stuff in her mouth. Grimacing, she turned her gaze to her special project, and the bad taste disappeared. Christmas cards were strewn across the right side of her desk. Some were very religious, with angels and wise men and stables. Some were whimsical, with animated reindeer, Santa in all sorts of situations, and several grinning mice. Then there were the more difficult kind. The ones with just words. Oh, sure, the calligraphy was always great, but how many Merry Christmases and Seasons Greetings could she put in her collage?

She popped a cube of cheese into her mouth and chewed it very slowly. She always ate slowly, and it drove her family nuts, but too bad. She wasn't ashamed of her eccentricities. They made her special.

"Girl, you *better* not let him see you messing with those cards."

Jane looked up to see Kadisha King, a friend from the secretarial pool, standing right next to her desk. Kadisha held a manila folder against her chest as if it were top secret. Jane hadn't even heard her approach. "It's Christmas."

"He doesn't care. Mr. Warren says no personal decorations at the desk, and that's what he means."

"Surely Christmas is an exception."

Kadisha shook her head in that knowing way of hers. "Fine. Do your paper dolls. But do you know how many personal assistants Mr. Warren has had in the last five years?"

Jane shook her head. She'd only been at Warren Industries for a year, and she wasn't very good at gossip.

"Eleven. You do the math." Kadisha tapped the manila folder with one perfectly manicured nail. Then she went to Delia's desk and put the folder in the in box.

Delia Robinson was Mr. Warren's executive assistant and she was on vacation until January 5, which meant that all the other secretaries had to work overtime. And that Jane got to see Mr. Charles Warren a whole lot more.

At the thought, the myriad cards on her right faded away. She continued to eat her food, but she didn't taste it. She might as well have had a sign around her neck: Preoccupied. Check Back in Ten Minutes. All she could see was Charles. Her poor, sweet, misunderstood Charles.

He smiled at her in that adorable, gruff way. A stranger would have thought nothing of it, but Jane...she knew the smile was an extraordinary event. It was filled with love, with mischief, with gratitude. Charles said it himself—what would he do without her?

He turned to their Christmas tree, a massive Douglas fir fit for the White House, and put an ornament on a limb. She shook her head, teasing him gently, then moved the ornament up half an inch.

"Of course," Charles said, his voice filled with adoration and admiration. "That's the perfect spot. I never would have seen it. Is there nothing you can't do?"

She blushed demurely, which always drove Charles wild. He pulled her into his arms and—

The buzz, so loud it probably woke up half of New Jersey, slashed through her daydream. She looked down to find nothing but orange peel on her napkin. Hmm. She didn't remember anything past peeling. But there was no time to wonder about all that.

Grabbing her notebook, she dashed past Delia's fortress of a desk to Mr. Warren's office. Before she entered the great man's domain, she straightened her skirt—tartan, on sale at Barneys for twenty-two dollars, and you couldn't even see the stain. She adjusted her mohair sweater, five dollars at Goodwill, thank you very much. And of course, she made sure her tartan beret was at the perfect jaunty angle. When she was certain everything was tip-top, she knocked quietly on the thick wooden door, then stepped through the portal.

It wasn't until she was inside that she remembered to check her teeth for lipstick. She closed the door behind her as quietly as she could, then nonchalantly ran a finger quickly over her teeth. Good. He hadn't seen. In fact, he hadn't looked at her at all.

She headed for his massive teak desk, so highly shined it was almost a mirror. With each silent step across the thick gray carpet her heart pounded harder in her chest. The closer she got, the more difficult it was to breathe. Luckily, even when she was as close as she could get, she was really quite far from the man himself. You could land a plane on this desk. "Yes, sir?"

He didn't look up for a long moment. Long enough for her to drink in the sight of him. He wasn't classically handsome; his face was too flawed for that. But it was the flaws that drew her to him. The slightly crooked nose, the small scar on his forehead. His eyes were perfect, however. Dark brown, penetrating. Captivating. And when he smiled it was sheer heaven. He wasn't terribly tall, maybe six feet, but he had one of those wiry, strong bodies. She'd seen his bare arms once, when he'd rolled up his sleeves. They were corded with muscle and sinew and had been a major part of her dreams ever since.

"I need you to take some dictation."

She jumped, but just a little. "Yes, sir," she said as

she went to the small chair in front and to the right of the desk. She crossed her legs, making sure her skirt crawled up her thigh so much and no more. Then she put her pad on her knee and smiled brightly. He just kept reading the papers on his desk.

"Take this down exactly—Holly Baskin, late of Vassar, call C.W."

Jane looked up, pen poised. "Go on."

"There is no more. I want you to type that up and, first thing tomorrow morning, take it to the offices of *Attitudes* magazine. I want it in the December 18 issue."

"In the personals?"

"Yes."

"Holly Baskin?"

He spelled both names slowly. Then he looked at Jane. Maybe *glanced* would be a better word. But there was no fooling her. She'd seen the unmistakable passion in his dark, dark eyes. He loved her. He *did*. He just didn't know it yet.

So, who was Holly Baskin? Why would Charles, of all people, have to find her in the personal ads? At least *Attitudes* was an upscale magazine, glossy and terribly hip—must-have reading for those in the know. The ads ran to Beemers and PalmPilots. But the real popularity of the magazine was in "The Personal Touch," the column where twice every month, Gen Xers paid $4.98 to find love, spurn love, make friends, blast friends. The city had been enamored with "The Personal Touch" for years now, some people making it their goal in life to have the coolest ad. Jane bought the magazine from time to time, when she could afford it, and, after she'd read the ads, she'd cut out pictures of things she wanted for her dream home.

But that wasn't important now. The ad was. Holly Baskin. Was she an old friend? From his Harvard days, perhaps? Maybe she was a business associate. A lover? Oh, please, not that.

Jane studied Charles, searching for clues. Nothing. His gaze was inscrutable. Beautiful, yes, but still not easy to read.

"Ms. Dobson?"

"Yes?"

"Why are you still here?"

She snapped out of it, trying like hell to look as if she hadn't been caught with her pants down, so to speak. Giving him one of her best smiles, she got up and backed away until her butt hit the door. His gaze stayed on her as she fumbled with the knob, then dropped her pad, but halfway to picking it up, he went back to his papers. She scurried out, closed the door and sagged against the frame.

Not a particular success, that. He rattled her so. Of course, he hadn't meant to. It was her own fault, really. But couldn't he just once smile?

As she headed back to her desk she glanced down at the name on her notepad. Holly Baskin. *Holly*. It didn't seem the kind of name Charles would go for. With his firm footing in the world he needed a woman with a stronger name. A traditional name. Jane, for example.

The phone rang and she hurried the last few steps to her desk. "Mr. Warren's office."

"Hi, Janey."

"Oh, hi, Darra." Jane sat down, propping the note-book open before her. "How are you?"

"Great. Listen, I wanted to let you know that we're opening another restaurant three weeks from Sunday. It's not far from your office."

Jane put her pad facedown on the desk and gave her sister her whole attention. Darra never invited her to any of her celebrity-studded events. She and three other models, whose combined income could wipe out the national debt, had opened five restaurants, subtly named Haute Couture. They'd done so without Jane's attendance, so what was different this time?

"Jane? Are you there?"

"Yes."

"Okay. Would you like to come?"

"Me?"

"Of course you, silly. It's about time you saw what I've been up to."

"I've been to the restaurant in SoHo."

"You have?" Darra cleared her throat, but from her it sounded sophisticated, sexy even. "How did you like it?"

"It was nice. Very, uh, modern."

"Good. Now, I can mark you down as a definite?"

"I think so. What's the date?"

"December 23. It's a Sunday."

Jane had flipped the pages on her calendar to see that she had nothing jotted on the twenty-third. Or the whole week, for that matter.

"And Janey?"

"Yes?"

"Maybe you could, you know, ask your boss if he wanted to come, too. As our guest, of course."

A feeling as familiar to her as breathing hit her chest: disappointment, dark gray and sticky, her old friend, her childhood companion. It was as if she were full to bursting and empty, both at the same time. *Merry Christmas, Janey.* "Mr. Warren has a very busy schedule," Jane said, her voice not even hinting at her condition.

"But couldn't you even ask?"

"Why?"

"Because...because he's just the kind of clientele we're looking for. If he likes it, maybe he'll come back. And bring his friends."

"He won't."

"He won't what?"

"Be able to come. I just looked at his calendar. He'll be out of the country."

"Damn it."

"But I'll tell him about it when he comes back."

"Thanks," Darra said, and Jane could practically see her patented pout. It was a doozy of a pout, and it had made her sister a household name. Gorgeous Darra, whose face haunted Jane from billboards all over Manhattan.

"Put it there."

Jane almost asked her sister what she was talking about, but then she realized the comment hadn't been addressed to her. It was probably for Darra's boyfriend, Guy. He pronounced it "Gee," like some French baron or something when Jane knew perfectly well that he'd been raised in Omaha, Nebraska. Oh well.

Guy pronounced "Gee" went better with Darra, whose real name was Darlene.

"I gotta run, Janey. I'll talk to you soon."

"Bye," she said, but the phone cut her off. It wasn't that Darra meant to be mean. She really didn't. She just had this rather myopic view of the world. Copernicus be hanged; Darra was the center of the universe. At least when she wasn't around their other sisters.

The remarkable Dobson girls. Jane's eldest sister, Pru, had just finished a triumphant concert series with the Boston Symphony. Just days ago Jane had seen a little piece on her in the *Times*, about how her precious violin had been stolen. It turned up the next day, and Jane would bet the price of the Stradivarius that Pru had lost the damn thing. She was notorious for misplacing stuff.

Then there was Felicity. Two years younger than Pru, and already on the *USA Today* bestseller list. "The novelist of our generation," according to *People* magazine. All Jane knew was that Felicity hadn't answered her last three letters.

Darra came next. She'd started modeling at fourteen, and then there was that *Sports Illustrated* cover and she'd become a supermodel. As if *that* was a word.

Three incredible, beautiful, talented girls, all in a row. And then came Jane. Tone-deaf Jane. Moderately attractive Jane. Mediocre Jane, who was best known in New York society for not being her sisters. When she was mentioned, someone inevitably mentioned her hats.

Her hats.

With a deep sigh, Jane let go of her familial thoughts

and turned to something far more interesting. Holly Baskin. It was a puzzle worthy of a woman like herself. Who was this Holly Baskin? Why didn't Charles have her phone number? What part had she played in his past? Was she beautiful? Of course she was.

Jane typed the ad, printed it, took it back to her desk and decided it was all wrong. Holly wouldn't be intrigued enough by such a sterile request. What it needed was some pizzazz.

Her fingers flew across her keyboard as she typed and deleted and typed and deleted until she came up with the perfect ad. Not too much, not too little. Holly wouldn't be able to resist.

The phone book came out, and Jane called to get the address and hours for *Attitudes* magazine. Of course, she'd thought about placing the ad via phone or e-mail, but that was too impersonal. This was for Charles, and it had to be done exactly right. In person. Besides, she hadn't decided which ad to use, which was a major big deal.

After she hung up, she called the switchboard, alerting them to the fact that she would be an hour or so late tomorrow morning. And then she took both ads, his and hers, and put them in her purse. There was the afternoon to get through. She had some reports to type up and some filing to do. But first, she picked up her notepad one more time.

Holly Baskin. She didn't sound at all like someone Charles would love. But what if...?

AS SHE WAITED, Jane read her ad, then his ad, then her ad again. Hers was poetic, sincere, moving. His was bare and cold and clinical. She pictured herself as Holly Baskin, seeing the ad for the first time. The one in her left hand—the one Jane had written herself— would pique her interest instantly. No way would she overlook it. But his ad? No romance whatsoever. No promise of a sparkling future.

It was Jane's turn at the desk. The woman behind it didn't seem to like her job very much. She hadn't smiled once, barely spoke, and her brow seemed permanently furrowed.

"I'd like to place a personal ad, please."

The woman frowned. "You have it written out?"

Jane nodded, knowing she had to make her decision now. This instant.

"Well? I haven't got all day."

Jane knew her ad would bring Holly back into Charles's life. She knew it with absolute certainty.

She handed the woman the other ad.

She wasn't stupid, for heaven's sake.

THE DOW WAS DOWN five points and Charles had a headache. One was not caused by the other. It only seemed that way.

It was eleven-thirty. Maybe he should take some aspirin and call it a night. He eyed the paperwork strewn across his bed. If he quit now, he'd just have more to do in the morning.

He decided to go with the aspirin, however. Putting his lap desk to the side, he headed for the bathroom. Fourteen million for the Riverside complex, and that was just for starters. The architectural firm was a good one, the prospectus top-notch, and yet there was something about the deal that bothered him. Whatever it was, it had better come to the fore soon. The papers were due on the twenty-first.

He turned the light on in the bathroom and opened the medicine cabinet. The aspirin bottle shared space with antacids: chewable, caplet and liquid form. The rest of the cupboard was bare. The women in his life were always trying to fill this particular cabinet, and Charles had disposed of a plethora of miracle herbs, god-awful colognes and even the occasional feminine hygiene product. Finally, it appeared that his house-keeper had gotten the hint. And since she was the only woman currently in his life, he had his agreeably spare cabinet back.

He took three aspirin, turned off the light and went back to bed. MSNBC was still on, but it wasn't financial news. It took him a moment to get settled, then he started rereading the Riverside deal.

Not five minutes later, the phone rang. Charles sighed. There were only two people in the world who would call him at this hour. David, or his mother call-ing from the cruise ship. He hoped it was David.

"Darling, you'll never guess!"

"Hello, Mother."

"I won!"

"What did you win?"

"The costume contest. I was number one on the whole ship. It was a triumph. The applause... Oh, Charles I wish you could have been there."

"I wish I could have, too, Mother." His gaze fell on the thick file on his lap, then the clock. It was no use fighting it. He'd simply get up a half hour earlier tomorrow. He closed the file, then leaned back. "Tell me about it," he said.

His mother did just that. In excruciating detail. She'd worn her hair up and used a charming little Hermès scarf across her forehead to give her the look of a flapper. He heard about her dress, her bag, her shoes, her dinner. On and on. When she'd pause he'd say something. Nothing much, just an acknowledgment that he was indeed still there. Still listening.

But his mind did wander. Not too far, or she'd have guessed. Just to his day, then, naturally, to the decision he'd made last Friday. As his mother waxed lavish praise on the lobster claw hors d'oeuvres, he toyed with the idea of telling her. What an uproar he'd cause from here to the Caribbean. She'd tell him he mustn't go back to Holly. That he needed someone who had a heart. A soul. His mother was very big on souls.

What she didn't understand was that Holly was exactly what he needed. Her no-nonsense approach to life suited him. She knew how to entertain, and she was savvy enough about business to make any dinner conversation flow. She was attractive, she came from a good family. What he couldn't remember was exactly why they'd split up. It had been a few years. Probably something to do with his father's death. That had been a difficult time. But Charles had survived. He'd taken over the company. He'd taken over the care of his mother. Now it was time for the next phase. A wife. A child. He'd be thirty-two soon. By then, he wanted this marriage business over and done with.

It all depended on whether Holly still read that damned magazine. Why she'd left no forwarding address or phone number with her last landlord, he couldn't fathom. Her parents had died several years ago, and she had no siblings. He'd tried finding her through the alumni association, the Harvard club. He'd even called Le Cirque to ask the maître d' if he'd seen her.

The only information Charles had was that she'd been living abroad. Maybe she was back in the States, or maybe not. Wherever she was, she'd subscribe to *Attitudes*. When he'd known her, it had been her favorite reading material.

"Darling?"

"Yes, Mother?"

"You didn't answer me. Are you reading the *Wall Street Journal* while I'm talking to you?"

"No. Of course not. I was just distracted by this headache."

"Did you take something for it?"

"Yes."

"Chamomile tea will do wonders. You should brew some up right away."

"That's a great idea. As soon as we're done, I'll do just that."

Her sigh carried across the ship-to-shore phone line. "You won't. But I can't do anything about that, can I?"

"What do you mean?"

"I mean you think I'm a crackpot, with crackpot ideas. Imagine, winning a costume party at my age."

"If you like it, there's nothing wrong with it. You've earned your fun, Mother."

"I suppose. Kim and Molly are taking good care of me. You don't have to worry."

He winced. She wasn't supposed to know about Kim and Molly. They'd been hired to keep a discreet eye on his mother. They'd obviously done a poor job of it.

"It's all right," she said. "Stop pouting. You knew I would figure it out sooner or later. You're nothing if not predictable, Charles. Now go to bed. It's far too late for you to be up. You need to sleep."

"Good night, Mother."

"I'll call again soon."

He put the phone down and thought about opening the Riverside file again. For once, though, he obeyed his mother. He put away his reports and papers and headed off to brush his teeth. He must remember to set his alarm for four-thirty instead of five.

As he got down to the business of preparing for sleep, he tried to remember the specifics of his breakup with Holly. He'd instigated the proceedings, but for the life of him he couldn't remember why. It was probably nothing. Nothing at all. She'd make a fine mother to his children. A very capable wife. And, if his memory wasn't playing tricks on him, she was very capable in bed, too.

He just hoped she'd answer him soon, or he'd have to hire a private detective. Charles wanted to be married soon. If he couldn't find Holly, it would mean looking for someone new. The thought made him shudder.

It would have been so much easier for him if Mrs. Robinson hadn't gone off to Idaho for the holidays. Or was it Ohio? He didn't recall. His work was getting done, but everything took far more of his time than he cared to give. At least that girl—what was her name?

Joan? At least she had a firm grip on the English language, and she could spell. Granted, it wasn't much. But his luck with employees had never been stellar. For now, she'd do.

2

THE DAY THE AD CAME OUT, Jane got up with the sun. Streams of light flowed into the room, buzzing with tiny dancers, the flotsam and jetsam that filled the world and filled her with each breath. She liked knowing she had company all the time, even if it was microscopic.

Her dreams had been delicious, all about Charles and her. Her and Charles. The season had affected him, or was it just the nearness of her? Probably both. He'd been so tender.

Shivering in anticipation, she pushed off her blankets, all three of them, and sat up, her feet immediately searching for her fuzzy slippers. The floor was always painfully cold in the morning, dull wood that seemed to hug the chill like an old friend. But she couldn't afford to heat the place when she slept. Manhattan might be a magical city, but it was also expensive as hell. She could have mitigated her circumstances by sharing a room with, say, one or ten other people, but that wasn't for her. She needed her own space, and her little shoe box of an apartment was as private as could be.

Grabbing her robe from the end of the bed, she found her teeth clattering loudly as she headed for the bathroom. This was the worst place in the apartment. The coldest. But she'd worked out a system where her behind never had to actually touch the seat. Creative. That's what you needed to be in New York. Creative and warm-blooded.

After the loo, which sounded so much nicer to her ears than bathroom, she walked down the short hallway, eager to see her Christmas tree in the morning light. It was so beautiful. Not in the traditional sense, of course. But then, traditional beauty had never appealed to her.

She turned the corner and her gaze fell on the couch, covered with a wonderful old afghan that she'd found at a rummage sale to hide the aged patches and stains. Then the tree, her tree, listing a bit to the right, missing more needles than it should, but decorated with all the love and care she had in her. She'd made bows and sewn little hanging cloth baskets, which she'd filled with candy canes. And she'd made the most adorable fabric frame ornaments, putting a picture of someone she loved in each one.

Of course, Charles's picture was given the place of honor. Although none of the decorations would claim more than a nickel at the flea market, they meant a lot to her, and that was what really mattered, right?

So what if others couldn't see what she saw? So what if they thought she had a screw loose? Her vision held wonders, and that's what made it worthwhile to get up every morning.

It had always been like that. Her poor parents had never understood her. They'd had their nice Long Island life, filled with worries about the right schools and the right clothes and the right friends. Her mother had planned great things for her daughters, and only

Jane had disappointed. She'd tried to get through law school, honestly, but it wasn't her. She'd ended up daydreaming in class, getting into trouble. So what if she hadn't found her niche yet? There was still time, for heaven's sake. She was only twenty-six. She had her whole life in front of her.

Only, sometimes she worried that she was spending a little too much time thinking about Charles. Despite the way she looked at the world, she was just Jane, after all. Not Pru, not Felicity, not Darra. Just Jane. Maybe it would be more productive to daydream about men she stood a chance with.

She sighed as she stepped over to her kitchen counter, pressed the button on her coffeemaker, then leaned over the tiny table and turned on her shower. It actually wasn't bad, having the tub in the kitchen. She could cook breakfast and get clean at the same time. She wondered what Charles was doing now. As if it mattered. But still, what was the harm in wondering? Of course, his bathrooms would be extravagantly large. His kitchen bigger than her whole apartment. Not that she'd been to his place, but she knew him and his taste. It wouldn't surprise her if he had one of those bathtubs. You know, the kind with the steps and the Jacuzzi whirlpool nozzles?

She wandered over to the radiator and banged it a few times with a tire iron she'd found on Forty-second Street. The gurgle from the basement told her heat was on its meandering way. Then it was back to the shower, which would be warm enough by now. She tossed off her clothes and scurried into the tub, pulling the circular shower curtain around her.

Halfway through washing, she forgot the business with the tree. She forgot that she was just Jane. Instead, she was in the shower with *him*. He washed her hair with his long, strong fingers. Her knees grew weak as she leaned slightly back to feel his wet, warm body against her spine....

CHARLES ADJUSTED his gray silk tie, then picked up his hairbrush. The speakerphone in the bathroom hummed with white noise while he waited for David to come back on the line.

"You still there?"

"Yes." Charles finished the last of his ablutions. "And I'm leaving in about two seconds."

"Oh, keep your shorts on. It was an important errand."

"Your coffee?"

"Yes."

"For God's sake, David, you know—"

"I know you don't like distractions in the morning, but too bad. I need to know what you're doing on Christmas Eve."

"It's not for a week. I don't know yet."

"What do you mean, you don't know yet? Your life is planned so far in advance you probably know the day you're going to die."

"I don't know, David."

"Well, figure it out. Sarah wants you to come to dinner, and she won't leave me alone until I get it confirmed."

"Why don't you tell your sister she needs to get out more?"

"This from a man whose last date was what, a year ago?"

"David, I'm hanging up now."

"Wait. First tell me if today's the day."

"What are you talking about?"

"Does the ad come out today?"

"Yes."

"What are you going to do if she calls?"

"I'm going to answer the phone."

"Ha ha. Very amusing."

"I'm hanging up now."

"Don't you do it! Don't—"

He did. David would get over it. His former roommate and closest friend had several annoying habits, like calling in the morning when Charles needed the line free for his brokers. The Asian market didn't care about his Christmas plans, and neither, frankly, did Charles. The holidays were highly overrated and damned inconvenient. Business ground to a halt each year for the weeks before, during and after. But then, this year might be different. What he hadn't mentioned to David was that he hoped to be getting married during the lull. If Holly called. If she wasn't married already. If...

What the hell was he doing?

The thought came from nowhere, the words not even his. It was David in his head, warning him away from his very sensible plan. David, who thought his license as a psychiatrist gave him some kind of unique insight into the human condition. But David was a sentimentalist.

Still, the echo of a doubt lingered. Charles had never

figured out why he'd broken up with Holly. That was all. Once they met again, it wouldn't matter.

At least, he hoped it wouldn't matter. The last thing on earth he wanted to do was date. The mere word made him quake with dread. The fact was, he was bad at it. He didn't like to do things he was bad at.

He left the bathroom and found his breakfast on the dining room table: a six-minute egg, one slice of unbuttered toast and coffee. The *New York Times* was already laid out, courtesy of Ellen, his housekeeper, who was at that moment putting away dishes from the dishwasher.

"Morning, Mr. Warren," she said.

He nodded as he took his seat, then his gaze landed on the headlines. Ellen vanished as he started to read.

ONE CHICKEN LEG. Seven cashews. Three celery stalks. An apple. Half a sesame bagel. Excellent. Jane closed her lunch pail and flicked the lock into place. She'd go by the newsstand before she hit the subway. The ad was due out today. A shiver of apprehension raced up her spine when she thought about Holly Baskin. Would she read the magazine? Would she look in the personals? Would she call?

As Jane trotted down all six flights of stairs leading to the street, she wondered yet again if she should have substituted her want ad for his. She didn't like to think of herself as selfish. But then, Charles didn't even know she'd written an alternate ad, so where was the harm? She'd done as he'd requested. Period. No explanations would be needed.

Even though she hadn't done anything wrong, she

still felt guilty. Not robbing-a-bank guilty, but enough
to make her uncomfortable. If she really loved him, she
would have substituted her ad for his. Because with
real love, you're supposed to care more for the other
person than you do for yourself, right?

She did love him, that much she knew. But sometimes it wasn't easy. He was so busy. Under such
stress. He worked too hard, that's for sure. And he
laughed way too seldom.

She walked out onto the street and pulled on her
gloves as she headed toward the corner. The snow under her feet had turned mushy and brown, slippery,
too. It was a good thing she'd left a few minutes early.
Charles hated anyone being late. It was really a thing
with him. It wouldn't do her a bit of good to use getting
his magazine as an excuse. Lateness, according to
Charles, had no excuse.

At least she had time to look at the Christmas decorations in the windows. Her mother was appalled that
she lived in Harlem, positive Jane would end up dead
in some alley, but her mother didn't understand Brand
Avenue. Although Jane hadn't met many of her neigh-
bors, the ones she did know were as nice as they could
be. Mrs. Franklin, who lived over the butcher shop,
had helped her find some gorgeous velvet once, which
Jane had used to make her favorite purse. Teddy at the
newsstand sometimes liked to talk about books. Very
nice people, indeed. *Real* people.

Even the butcher shop looked festive this morning
with all its pretty decorations. The dead chickens hanging in the window almost looked like reindeer.

"Good morning, Miss Jane."

"Hi, Teddy. How are you?"

The older man, she had no idea how old, shook his head. "Not great, Jane. Not great."

"What's wrong?"

"Nothin' but old. Old hurts."

"It doesn't have to. I know you don't eat well, and I'll wager you don't take any vitamins, either."

"Vitamins? Are you crazy? You don't know what they put in them things. They're hauling pills off the counters every day."

"You're talking about herbs. I'm talking One-A-Day multiples."

"The only thing I need once a day is a piece of apple pie."

"My point exactly."

He grinned at her, at the argument they'd had a hundred times. She wished he would take better care, though.

"What can I get you today?"

"I need a copy of *Attitudes*."

"That all?"

"That's all."

He gave her the magazine and she gave him five dollars. When he turned to ring up her change, she darted away. "Hey!"

"Have a good day!" she called over her shoulder. Then she waved as she walked down the subway steps.

CHARLES UNLOCKED his office door, then flipped on the light switch. He liked being the first one in. Normally, Mrs. Robinson would have been here, would have had his coffee ready along with his agenda. But he wasn't helpless. He knew how to make coffee, and he knew how to work a calendar. He missed his routine, that's all. He liked it when the world worked like a well-oiled machine.

He put his briefcase down, then took off his coat and his kidskin gloves. Ben, his driver, had had to drop him off down the street this morning, and Charles's shoes had paid the price. The construction on the building had become increasingly annoying, and he wished they'd finish. It wasn't going to happen anytime soon, though, so he'd better make a note to wear his galoshes for a while.

In the meantime, he had to go to his washroom and work for a considerable time to repair the damage to the Italian leather. When he finished, he made coffee, and the moment he turned on the machine, the phone rang.

For Charles, the sound was like the gun at the start of a race, sending him into his day. It would be Frank Toyamichi calling from Japan. Charles had an appointment with Bob Riverside and his people at nine. Lunch, as usual, at Charlemagne. His attorneys were due this afternoon, and tonight David was taking him to an auction at Christie's where he hoped to purchase a rocking chair that had once belonged to Jack Kennedy.

"Charles Warren," he said into the speaker phone as he settled into his chair.

"Mr. Warren. It's Frank. I have the numbers for you."

Charles glanced at the clock. It was exactly seven-fifteen. Frank was a good man. A punctual man. Charles liked things punctual.

SHE WAS LATE. The subway train had been delayed more than ten minutes several miles before her Wall Street station. She'd passed the time reading the magazine in her lap, returning again and again to the personals. To the unadorned ad. "Holly Baskin, late of Vassar, call C.W."

Holly. Certainly an appropriate name for the season. She'd be blond, of course. Or maybe her hair would be chestnut. Those Vassar girls liked chestnut.

She'd be beautiful, too. Slender, with good ankles and perky B cups. She'd have impeccable taste in all things. She'd know the right restaurants, the right wine, the right jewelers, the right people. She'd be the perfect complement to everything that Charles was. Only...

Only she wouldn't love him the way Jane did. She couldn't. If she had, she never would have left him. Not for anything. Only a fool would leave Charles Warren.

Holly wouldn't understand his need for laughter. She wouldn't see that his was a cautious soul that needed lots of loving care. Poor Charles didn't want anyone to see his vulnerability, and Holly, who might be very attractive and speak umpteen languages, was too selfish to look beyond the facade. The only one, Jane thought, who had an inkling about the real Charles was David Levinson. He came to the office a couple of times a month, and he never failed to ask her how she was, and about her latest project. He was so nice. Such a sweetie pie. He never rushed his conversations, even if Charles tried to hurry him up.

She could see that David was worried about Charles, just as she was. And that David wasn't having any luck getting Charles to see he had to slow down. But then, David was just a friend. Not a girlfriend. Not a wife.

The train started with a jerk and before she had a chance to fix her lipstick, she arrived at Pearl Street. Jane hustled out with about a million other people who were just as late as she was. No one spoke to each other, no one looked at each other. As far as she could see in this mass of humanity, there wasn't one smile.

It was too near Christmas for such dour moods. She wished she was brave enough to say something. Just to holler, "Lighten up!" But then someone shoved her in the back, and she nearly stumbled. She sighed. Sometimes it was difficult to keep a positive attitude.

On the street, she breathed in a healthy dose of fresh air. But there was no time to appreciate the morning smells of doughnuts and coffee coming from the cart next to her. She had to run if she was going to make it to the office on time.

She dashed across the street with all the other pedestrians, dodging taxis and limos. The chorus of horns was anything but festive. She didn't understand the honking. It never changed anything. Maybe all those drivers were just trying to be heard. A primal cry, desperate in its futility.

One of those desperate souls nearly ran her over, and she teetered on the edge of the sidewalk for a moment. No one noticed.

She walked as quickly as she dared, nearing the

huge office building in the heart of Wall Street. Some-where among all the noise and hubbub she heard the jingle of a bell. A street-corner Santa. That made things a little easier to take.

One more street crossed, and then she was under the scaffolding, pushing through the throng of office work-ers huddled in their heavy coats, their gloved hands thrust in pockets or gripping briefcases.

Again she was bumped. A man on a cell phone. Just as she was about to give him a piece of her mind, a scream, "Watch out!" made her look up.

Something was falling—

It hit her on the head. White light filled her vision and agony turned her legs to mush. Then the white faded to black, and that was all.

HER HEAD HURT. When she opened her eyes, the light hurt, too. "Ouch."

"Good, you're awake."

"Huh?" She blinked, trying to figure out who was talking to her. A man in a coat. A white coat.

"You're in an emergency room. I'm Dr. Larson. You were hit on the head."

"I was?" She touched her forehead gingerly, but all she felt was a bandage.

"It's amazing you're alive. That was quite a blow."

"What was?"

"This," he said, holding up a plaster statuette. After a long moment she realized it was a Cupid. Complete with bow and arrow. Except the right wing was broken and his feet were missing.

"I was hit in the head by *Cupid?*"

"By about two pounds of plaster."

"Am I all right?"

"I don't know yet. Let's find out, shall we?"

She nodded. Big mistake. Her head throbbed with an ungodly pain, the worst she'd ever felt. For a moment, the blackness threatened. She clung to something cold as steel as she struggled to focus her vision.

The doctor's concerned look didn't help matters any. Maybe she was really hurt. Seriously hurt. "It's all right," she said finally, knowing that it wasn't. "I'm okay."

"Why don't we let me be the judge of that?" He helped her sit, and it was then she realized she was on a gurney and her hand had been gripping the rail. Her skirt was torn and damp, her sweater dirty. The lump of black wool on the chair by the curtain must be her coat.

"Look at my finger."

She did, following the digit from right to left and back again. Then the doctor shone a light in her eyes, which made the throbbing worse.

When she could see again, she saw the doctor was young. Thirty? Maybe. Probably a resident. Or an intern. He was pretty good-looking, too. *Tres ER.*

His little rubber thingy hit her knee, and from the sound of the doctor's "humph" she gathered her reactions were normal. As he wrote on his clipboard, she noticed a little bit of shaving cream on his jaw just below his ear.

Her hand went to that spot on her own face, hoping he'd catch on. She didn't want to tell him. He seemed very nice, but also shy, and she had the feeling he would be embarrassed.

"All right, then. Let's move on. What's your name?"

Her gaze jerked up, making her wince. Her name. *Her name.* Why on earth couldn't she think of it? "That's odd."

"What?"

"Uh..."

"Yes?"

"Well. Um, I can't seem to recall."

"You can't seem to recall what?"

She smiled. Laughed, although it really wasn't funny. "My name."

His whole body language changed from relaxed to red alert. "I see," he said, failing to calm her with his words.

"You see what?" Her stomach clenched and it suddenly was hard to breathe. She recognized the signs of a panic attack, and she hadn't had one in years. Why did she know *that*, and not her name?

"What's your mother's name?"

Nothing came. Her mind was a blank.

"Brothers, sisters? Your father?"

She closed her eyes, focusing every ounce of her energy on not screaming.

"You didn't come in with a purse. And there was nothing in your pockets."

His voice faded a bit, and when she opened her eyes again he was standing by her coat.

"This was in your hand." He held up a glossy magazine. *Attitudes.*

And then it hit her. She nearly swooned with relief.
"Oh, thank God."

"Yes?"

"I remember. Of course. Wow, that was scary."

"What is it?"

"My name?"

He nodded.

"It's Holly. Holly Baskin."

3

LARRY PODESKY, Bob Riverside's attorney, wetted the tip of his finger slowly, then used that finger to turn to the next page of the legal brief. He went on reading line by painful line in a voice better suited to mortuary work than high finance. The mildly disturbing tableau wasn't enough, however, to focus Charles.

The damn girl hadn't even called. That's what got him. The simple courtesy of a phone call this morning and everything would have been fine. He'd have had time to get a suitable temp, someone who knew how to make palatable coffee, who wouldn't spill water all over Riverside's pants. Things would have gone according to plan.

"...the party of the first part, will make appropriate restitution to landowners..."

Charles tried to focus on the contract, but his attention was waylaid by four drops of water on the conference table. Remnants of the mishap of an hour ago, they were perfect bubbles, contained within themselves, shimmering when Podesky jostled the table. For God's sake, millions of dollars were at stake, and he was busy thinking about beads of water. He dismissed them, turned his attention to the pages before him, but every few words his gaze would dart over to the drops. It was all he could do not to leap out of his chair and blot the water before it could torment him further.

Damn it. Podesky might as well have been speaking Greek. Charles couldn't listen, hadn't been able to listen from the start.

He'd have to postpone his decision, that's all. Which wasn't a bad idea when he thought about it. Something was amiss here, and in his distraction, the only hint he'd had was the fact that Riverside's face was a dull pink. Not just some of his face. All of it had a distinct rosy hue. Having met Riverside several times before, Charles knew this wasn't the man's normal complexion. The temperature in the office was a cool seventy-two, so what was making the man so nervous?

Charles was pleased he'd thought to do a little digging into Riverside's past. If there were skeletons to be found, his man Sterling would find them. The importance of today was to listen well, get his own take on the man and the deal.

Unfortunately, he'd failed miserably on both accounts.

"...two-hundred seventy thousand dollars, to be held at Chase Manhattan Bank until such t—" Podesky stopped midword as his gaze jerked to the door of the conference room. Riverside followed suit and reacted with an open mouth and widening eyes.

Charles spun in his chair to see what the hell—

Ms. *Dobson? Joan* Dobson? With a white bandage on her forehead? With a dirty, torn skirt and blouse? With only one shoe?

She swept into the room like a strong gust of wind,

heading straight for him. Her arms spread expansively and a smile lit her smudged face. "Charley!"

Charley?

She swooped down on him, giving him no chance to escape, and for a moment he wondered if she was going to kill him. It was obvious she'd gone off the deep end. He tensed, but instead of a knife in his ribs, he got a kiss on the mouth.

He would have preferred the knife.

She kissed him deeply, her full lips squarely on his, her body bent at such an angle that his head was forced back against his leather chair. Her hands landed on his shoulders, the touch there almost as shocking and intimate as her kiss. That is, until he felt the unmistakable wetness of her tongue.

He opened his mouth to protest, but a second later he realized his error. Her tongue, *Ms. Dobson's tongue*, slipped into his mouth. Searching, teasing, it moved sinuously against his teeth, his own tongue. The indecency, the impudence shocked him so fiercely that he forgot how to breathe.

He moved his head, but she moved with him, a low rumble from her throat making it sound as if his attempt at escape was something entirely different. As if he'd moved to please her.

His hands found her shoulders somehow, and he pushed her back, but not before she nipped his lower lip. She straightened slowly, her smile mischievous, her eyes alight with what Charles could only guess was insanity. She must have been in a terrible accident that had caused her to lose all sense of propriety.

"I saw it, Charley," she said, her intimate whisper

sending aftershocks through his body. "I saw the personals. It was so clever of you to think of that. You knew I'd read it, didn't you? And you knew I'd drop everything to be with you."

He opened his mouth as he struggled to understand. But before he was able to say a word, she'd turned to Riverside and his attorney.

"Please forgive my intrusion," she said. "But love makes for foolish choices sometimes. You see, Charley and I, we're going to be married."

Riverside cleared his throat. "Pardon?"

She laughed, the sound so out of place Charles wondered if he was dreaming. "I'm Holly Baskin," she said as she walked around the table to where Riverside sat. "I know I must look terrible, but I couldn't wait to get here. In fact, I left everything behind." She turned to Charles, and the way she looked at him sent a shiver of fear down his spine. "I'll need to get some things, sweetie, if you don't mind."

Holly Baskin? What in hell...? He shook his head, wondering if he should call the police or Bellevue or both. David. David would know what to do. He dealt with crazy people all the time.

Ms. Dobson sighed, her gaze all moony, like a lovesick calf. On the other hand, maybe that's what people looked like when they were about to go over the edge. He opened his mouth to order her out of his office, but before he could say the first word she'd dashed to him once more, her blond curls bobbing merrily. Why had she said she was Holly? Blackmail? Dementia? Worse?

"I've got to go get something decent to wear, but

then I'll meet you at your place later. We have so much to talk about."

He leaned forward.

She bent over him, stealing his protest with another kiss.

The next second she straightened, smiled, then she was out the door. He should follow her. See that she didn't steal anything, shoot anyone, jump out any windows. At the very least he should be on the phone with the police. But that last kiss...

It had *affected* him. Embarrassingly. Visibly. If he stood...

He shifted his chair up against the conference table. Riverside and his attorney stared at him with unabashed shock. Riverside's once pink hue was now closer to scarlet, and Podesky's papers had fallen off the table.

Charles cleared his throat. Then again. "I'm sorry about that, gentlemen."

Riverside looked at him, then at the door, then back again. "Your fiancée?"

"No. No, not at all. She's my assistant."

Podesky's right brow rose.

"And her name isn't Holly Baskin."

"I see," Riverside said, even though it was obvious he didn't see. But then, Charles didn't see, either.

"Uh, gentlemen, I think it would be best if we rescheduled."

Podesky nodded, then bent over to get his file. Riverside just kept looking at him. Charles wanted them out, gone. He needed to calm down. To think this through. He needed to talk to David.

An electronic buzz made him jump, which wasn't nearly as bad as what happened to Podesky. He not only dropped the file again, but the back of his head banged viciously against the bottom of the table when he reached for it.

Charles pressed the intercom. "Yes?"

"Uh, Mr. Warren?" the secretary said, her voice tentative and so soft he barely made out the words.

"Yes?"

"Uh, I think you'd better come out here."

He let go of the button. The interruption had cleared his head a bit, and it had also managed to take care of his other problem, at least most of the way. He stood, pulled his cuffs down, straightened his tie, then faced Bob Riverside. "Pardon me."

"Oh, sure," Riverside said, although he still sounded dazed.

Charles left, trusting the men would see themselves out. But he didn't head toward the outer office. Instead he took advantage of the empty hallway and regrouped. He couldn't be rash. In today's climate, it wasn't safe to make a move without attorneys and human resources. If he fired her on the spot, there might be repercussions. On the other hand, she was a loon.

After a steadying breath, he entered the outer office. Ms. Dobson wasn't there. The woman who was today's replacement for Delia Robinson—he'd completely forgotten her name—seemed dazed. Her chair had been pushed back from the desk to make room for the open top drawer.

"I tried to stop her," she said.

"Stop her from what?"

The woman blinked rapidly behind bottle-thick glasses, then tried to smile. "She said it was all right. That you wouldn't mind."

He headed toward the desk, struggling to keep his composure. Ayres. That was her name. "Ms. Ayres, what, precisely, happened?"

"She took the credit card. And some keys. I didn't even know they were there. I swear. I never opened that part of the desk."

"My credit card?"

Ms. Ayres nodded. She was young, almost as young as Ms. Dobson. He thought she might cry.

"Please find the number for David Levinson. Call him and put it through to my office."

"Yes, Mr. Warren," she said, her voice a little wobbly.

"And after that, please bring me three aspirin and a glass of water."

"Yes, Mr. Warren," she repeated, this time with a definite tremor.

"And Ms. Ayres?"

"Yes, Mr. Warren?"

"It's all right. I don't hold you responsible."

"Thank you, Mr. Warren."

He headed for his office, wondering what in hell he was supposed to do now. Call the credit card company, of course, and then...?

After closing the door behind him, he paused. Something was bothering him, aside from the obvious. She'd called herself Holly Baskin. Today was the day the ad was supposed to come out in that damn magazine. Had she gone to pick up a copy and been hit by a car? Had she been mugged? Or was it possible that this was just some horrible prank?

His phone rang and that got him moving. He answered as he sank into his chair. "Warren."

"What's up?"

"David, I've got a situation."

"Shoot."

"Don't say that. Please."

"Okay." David's voice had changed. It was subtle, but Charles knew him so well that he noticed the nuance. David was now sitting up straight at his desk. He had stopped fiddling with his paper clips. He was focused, and no one was smarter than David when he was focused.

"You know my assistant."

"Delia?"

"The other one."

"Jane?"

"I thought her name was Joan."

"It's Jane."

"Oh. Well. Jane, then. She wasn't in this morning."

"Oh?"

"I had to use someone from the secretarial pool. She made god-awful coffee."

"I assume this story is leading somewhere?"

"Right. I was in the middle of a meeting with Riverside and his attorney, and this girl, this Jane, barged in. Just walked into the conference room like she owned the place."

"Really?"

"She had a big bandage on her forehead. She looked

as though she'd been in an accident. Or perhaps she'd been mugged. I'm not sure."

"Did you call a doctor?"

"No."

"Why not?"

"Because she—"

"Yes?"

"She kissed me."

"Pardon?"

"She kissed me. On the lips. In the conference room. She said she was Holly Baskin. That we were going to be married."

Silence. No, not quite. Was that a muffled laugh? A slight tap on his door heralded Ms. Ayres and his aspirin, and Charles had swallowed the pills before David spoke again.

"This is a little tricky," he said, finally.

"I know that. What I need to know is what to do. The woman took my credit card. God knows what she's charging. I have to call the—"

"Don't."

"What?"

"Don't call the police or anyone else. Not yet."

"Why not?"

"Because we need more facts before we do anything."

"Facts? I'll give you a fact. A crazy woman is out in the city with my credit card."

"Did she say anything?"

"Yes."

"What?"

"She said she had to pick up a few things and that... Oh, God."

"What?"

"She said she'd meet me at my place. She took my keys, too."

"Okay. So that's where we'll start."

Charles heard papers shuffling. He wondered if he'd explained the seriousness of the situation adequately. The woman was nuts, and she had his credit card and the key to his home. And yet David didn't seem unduly alarmed. In fact, his voice sounded utterly blasé when he said, "I'll cancel my three. You clear the deck on your end. I'll be at your place in half an hour."

"Fine. Good."

"And Charles?"

"Yes?"

"Order lunch, will you? I'm starving."

Before Charles had a chance to tell David his request was completely inappropriate, David hung up.

Charles did the same. His gaze wandered to his bookshelves. The neat, orderly rows, the fine leather bindings. He liked the look of them, always had. He'd meant to go through them. Just last...last year he'd decided to go back to reading something other than the *Wall Street Journal*. He hadn't, of course. The year had gone by in a blur of deals, of business lunches, of NASDAQ ups and downs. The company had grown, and the shareholders were going to see some healthy dividends. It was all as it was supposed to be. Only—

He shook himself out of his reverie and pressed the button for Ms. Ayres. He had to cancel his afternoon. All because of one little slip of a girl. He never should have hired her. Those curls of hers were a dead give-away. She was trouble. Big trouble.

"I THINK WE SHOULD CALL the police."

David shook his head. "It's only four-thirty. Let's give it till five."

"By five, she could have wiped out Saks."

"Charles, let me ask you something." David leaned forward and pushed aside his beer so he could rest his hands on the dining room table. "Have you ever spoken to Jane?"

"Of course. She works for me."

"I mean, have you spoken to her in a nonbusiness context?"

"No. Why would I?"

"Because you see her five days a week."

"David, I don't go in for that touchy-feely crap, and you know it."

"I'm not asking if you've hugged her lately, just if you've talked. If you know anything about her."

Charles massaged his temples, wondering what would happen if he took three more aspirin. Or maybe he should just have a drink. "I only know that up until today, she'd done an adequate job."

"Have you ever heard of Pru Dobson?"

"The violinist?"

David nodded. "That's Jane's eldest sister."

"Didn't we see her play?"

"We did."

"Hmm."

"And have you heard of Felicity Dobson?"

"The name rings a bell, but—"

"The novelist."

"Right."

"Also Jane's sister."

"Really."

"And maybe you've heard of Darra Dobson?"

He shook his head.

"Turn around."

"What?"

"Just turn around."

Charles obeyed, swiveling to face the window of his tenth-floor penthouse.

"See the billboard next to the Chivas Regal whiskey sign?"

He nodded. It was huge, hardly something he could miss, even if he wanted to. A seminaked woman stared hungrily at a seminaked man. She wore his underwear. He didn't appear to be wearing anything except a smile.

"That's Darra Dobson. Jane's other sister."

"No kidding?"

"No kidding."

Charles turned back. "Remarkable."

"Yes. Four girls. Three of them international celebrities."

"And then Jane."

David nodded.

"That's very touching, but what does it have to do with me?"

"I'm not sure yet. But I think your Ms. Dobson is in trouble."

"So what am I supposed to do about it?"

"I'll let you know when I figure it out."

"I think this is a matter for the authorities, David."

"Not yet. Not until I speak with her."

"She's probably on a plane to Monte Carlo."

He shook his head, propped his fingers in a steeple and peered over the top. "No. I don't think so. I think she'll be back."

"David, I know what your grade point average was, so knock it off."

"Knock what off?"

"Your Freud imitation."

"I'm not the one who called looking for help, buddy boy."

Charles sighed. "I know. I just—"

The sound of a key opening the dead bolt made both men jump. Charles looked at David. David looked at the door.

David stood. Charles didn't.

Jane Dobson waltzed in and dropped several beige bags as she kicked the door shut behind her. The bandage was gone, revealing a considerable goose egg. She'd changed into decent, expensive looking clothes, and she had two shoes.

"Hello, Charley," she said. "Hi, David."

David nodded. "Hi."

"What? No kiss?"

David shot Charles a quick glance, then smiled at Jane. He took her outstretched hands, then kissed her on the cheek. "You look wonderful."

"Thanks. So do you. Did he tell you?"

"What?"

"That we're getting married."

"He mentioned it, yes."

"Thrilling, isn't it?"

"I'll say."

She let go of David's hands and headed toward Charles. She was going to kiss him again, he just knew it. But this time, she'd get no reaction from him. None at all. The girl needed help. She was ill. Or psychotic.

She bent over him.

She smelled like roses.

4

IT WASN'T AS IF SHE HAD a choice. He was so delicious, and she'd loved him for so long. Adorable, stuffy Charley. Sweet, tender Charley. Holly leaned that last inch, her eyes fluttered closed and her lips touched his.

The same jolt of awareness, the same surge of emotion washed through her, scary and oh, so wonderful. She wished she wasn't in such an awkward position. What she wanted was to be in his arms, in his bed. She couldn't wait for the wedding. But maybe she didn't have to.

She stood up, leaving Charley agape, his startled expression cute as a button. "I have some things being delivered," she said, "but they won't be here for a little while. In the meantime, I thought we might talk about the wedding. I've found the perfect place, if they have a room." She shook her head. "You didn't give me much notice, Charley."

"Didn't what?"

David coughed. "He meant for the date to be a surprise. So how did you figure it out, you clever girl? Were you doing a little snooping?"

She shook her head. She hadn't. At least, she didn't think she had. So how did she know? Love, that was it. She loved him, and that gave her special insight. "I know everything about Charley. I know he likes to come into the office early, so that he can get a jump on his day. He clears his throat whenever he needs to re-group, or find just the right word."

She turned to Charles and looked into his beautiful face. "Sometimes, when he thinks no one's looking, he takes his shoes off behind his desk. And sometimes, when he's alone, he talks to his father."

Charley's eyes widened until she thought he might hurt himself. And his color was none too good, either.

"Now, why are you so surprised, silly? When two people love each other like we do, it's only natural that we know each other's secrets. I bet you know all of mine."

He looked from her to David, then back again. The tops of his ears reddened. He was shy. Oh, God, it was so darling. So *Charley.*

David moved to Charley's side. "He knows you like to sew. And how much you love those Stephen Sondheim musicals."

Holly's insides melted. "Oh, Charley, it's true. We are meant for each other. Even time and distance couldn't pull us apart." She leaned toward him again, but a knock on the door interrupted. "Wait till you see what I got."

She ended up giving him a quick kiss on the chin, then she rushed to the door. The doorman was there along with two other gentlemen. All three were loaded down with packages.

"Come this way," she said, waving them in. She crossed the living room, then paused for a moment. Funny, she couldn't remember which way to turn. She must be overexcited, that's all.

She held up a finger to stop the parade. "One sec." The first door on her right was a bathroom. The second door was the bedroom. "Back here!"

The room was very large, big enough to make the king-size bed seem small. But the colors were all wrong. Dark browns, hunter green, black. Ugh. Depressing. She'd have to do something about that, and quick.

The closet was gigantic, with three walls of perfectly spaced clothes, mostly suits, shirts, dress slacks, all color coordinated. But there was one pair of jeans and three pairs of khakis. The poor dear didn't have the first clue about having fun. But then, that was her job, wasn't it?

The men arrived, spurring her into action. She pushed a whole rod of suits together, then started transferring the clothes to the middle wall.

"In here."

The doorman ushered in the other two men.

"Just put the boxes on the floor," she said. "I'll take it from here."

"Yes, ma'am." The doorman deposited his stack first, then kept an eye on the others as they did the same. He ushered them out with a touch of his cap.

"Mr. Warren will see to the tip," she said, then she faced the clothes racks once more. She'd definitely need more space for shoes. And where in heaven's name was she supposed to put her hats?

DAVID COUGHED. When that didn't work, he gave Charles an elbow to the ribs. "They're waiting for a tip," he whispered.

"They're what?"

"Just hand them each ten dollars."

"I most certainly will—"

David smiled at the doorman and his cohorts as he reached into his own pocket. He pulled out three tens and gave one to each of the men. After three quick nods, they walked to the door single file, and then were gone. David felt Charles's stare boring into his back. He turned, prepared for the onslaught.

"What in hell do you think you're doing?"

"Saving your ass."

"What?"

"Sit down, Charley."

"Don't call me that."

"Fine. Sit down, Charles." David went back to the dining room chair he'd been in before, and finally, after a heated glare, Charles took his old seat.

"Well?"

"The girl is obviously in trouble."

"I don't need you to tell me that. It's crystal clear she's in trouble. The murky part is why we haven't called the police."

"The police?" David shook his head slowly, desperately searching for a way to carry out his plan. Granted, it was bold. Probably unethical. Definitely insane. But it felt right. Incredibly right.

"Yes. The police."

"I wouldn't advise it."

"Why not?"

"She was on the clock, Charles."

"So?"

"So it's a workman's comp issue. And you're liable."

"Don't I pay insurance for this kind of thing? Let the attorneys handle it."

"That's one way to go, I suppose."

Charles looked at him through narrowed eyes. Nothing about his expression indicated he trusted David worth spit, but at least he hadn't picked up the phone.

"And the other would be what, exactly?"

"Play along with her," he said, diving in before Charles decided enough was enough. "With amnesia like this, you have to tread delicately if you don't want her to suffer permanent damage."

"So you're saying we need to take her to the hospital."

"No. What I'm saying is that you have an opportunity to do something nice for her."

"What are you talking about?"

David knew he was playing dirty, but he wasn't going to think about that right now. "This is the kind of thing we might expect from your mother. You know how she is. And if it did happen to your mother, you'd want the people she was with to be patient and kind, wouldn't you?"

Charles's right brow rose. "Then why don't we call her family?"

"I'm going to. They'll probably be here in an hour or two. Surely you can watch her until then."

"Watch her?"

"Right. Humor her. Just pretend she's Holly."

"David, I have work to do. I can't be bothered with this nonsense."

"Right. I'm sorry. What was I thinking? Two hours out of your life—it's far too much to ask."

Charles cursed. And David knew he had him.

"So what do I have to do—exactly."

"Call her Holly. Pretend you are going to be married. Be affectionate. Listen to her."

"This is completely insane."

"No. It's not. In fact—" David lowered his voice "—Charles, this can go one of two ways. You play along, she comes out of it in a day or so, no harm, no foul. Or..."

"Or?"

"Or you call the police. They frighten her to death, making it impossible for her injured psyche to come back at all. Her family finds out, and I told you, this is some family. They'll have the best lawyers money can buy. They'll plaster this all over the papers. You'll be paying for her hospitalization the rest of her life, fighting court battle after court battle, and you know as well as I do that any jury of her peers is going to stick it right to you."

Charles's jaw flexed. He looked toward his bedroom, then back.

"But that's not the reason you need to do this." David wondered briefly if he had any business lying to Charles. But only briefly. Ever since his father's death, Charles had steadily lost his sense of humanity. He'd grown cold, bitter, too serious for his own good. He was headed in the same direction as his father, who'd died far too young. Something had to give. And that something was Jane Dobson-cum-Holly Baskin.

Charles closed his eyes for a moment, and when he

opened them again, David relaxed. Charles had given in that final inch. He'd still bitch like hell about it, but it was a done deal.

"You say it will only be a few hours?"

"Absolutely."

"What am I supposed to do with her?"

"Keep her here."

"What?"

"You don't want her out there, do you? You need to keep an eye on her until this is over."

"What about work?"

"What about it?"

"I can't be at work and watch her at the same time."

"Right. You have to make a decision. You can go to work, putting everything you own at risk, or you can stay home and protect the future of the company."

Charles cursed again. David scowled, even though he knew his victory was in the bag.

"I don't like this."

"Of course not. But you have an obligation to this girl. To yourself."

After a long, deep breath, Charles nodded. "I still think this is crazy."

"It's going to be fine. While you're watching her, I'm going to find out exactly what happened. And I'm going to contact her family."

"You're leaving?"

"I can't stay here. She'll get suspicious."

"But—"

"I've got my cell phone. If you need me, call me."

"*David...*"

He stood and put his hand on Charles's shoulder.

"You can do this. It won't be easy, but I know if anyone can pull this off, it's you."

"I hope so," he whispered.

David grabbed his coat and headed for the door, moving far more quickly than usual. "I'll call you," he said, then he stepped outside and closed the door behind him. He had to hustle to the elevator. It would blow everything if Charles saw his grin. The look on Charles's face! Priceless. God, to be a fly on the wall in that apartment tonight.

The elevator started down, but David's humor stayed on the tenth floor as he thought about Jane. He really was going to find out what had happened to her. From the looks of her, he didn't think she was too badly hurt physically. As for her mistaken identity? Jane was a dreamer. And he'd bet she always had been. That was what he liked most about her. His visits when he went to see Charles were always more interesting because of Jane. Long before this, uh, imbroglio, he'd thought Jane would be good for Charles. But there had never been a way to introduce the idea.

Charles had his feet buried ten feet in the ground, and Jane spent most of her days ten feet above it. They needed each other. *If* she was all right physically. If she didn't get her memory back in the next ten minutes.

He doubted that. She seemed to live more in her fantasies than in the real world, so it made a lot of sense that this would have occurred after an accident. She would come out of it relatively soon. He felt sure of that. Just, he hoped, not too soon.

The elevator came to a stop, and he wondered if

maybe he was risking too much. He got his cell phone out and hit speed dial 1. His secretary answered.

"Phyllis, I want you to do something for me."

"Yes, Doctor?"

"I want you to call all the hospitals near the Wall Street area. Find out if anyone had a Jane Doe this morning. A young woman, twenty-five or six. Blond hair, in unruly curls, blue eyes. Around five-three and slender, and she has a mouth no one would ever forget, so ask about that, all right? Oh, and she has a bruise and a large bump on her forehead."

"Yes, sir. And if I find the hospital?"

"Call me." He pressed the disconnect button and headed out of the building and down Fifth Avenue. The store windows were filled with toys, everything from Barbie dolls to diamond rings. The snow glistened on the sidewalks and the ledges, and somewhere bells were ringing.

He was a man of letters. A physician with two doctorates. He didn't, as a rule, believe in fate. But it was Christmas. And anything could happen at Christmas.

CHARLES STOOD HALFWAY between the front door and the bedroom. He'd never been one to run from a problem, but maybe this was a good time to change.

Jane Dobson. He tried to remember how she'd come to be his assistant. She had gone through the human resources department, of course, but at some point he had to have interviewed her.

Wait a minute. He did remember. Some of it, at least. He remembered thinking she had Kewpie doll lips. Deep red lipstick against her pale skin. Her lips had distracted him momentarily, and then there was something about her hair. As hard as he tried, he couldn't recall more. He needed details. Thank God David had told him a little bit about her. Her sisters—

Wait. She wasn't Jane Dobson. Not tonight. She was Holly, but not the Holly he knew. Which left him where?

The front door was looking awfully good.

He winced at the sound of something large hitting the floor in his bedroom. It could be anything. His fax machine. His laptop. Oh, hell, it might be *her*.

He headed for his room, praying she hadn't fallen. Or fainted. Or worse. By the time he stepped inside, his hands were damp and his blood pressure was through the roof.

Nothing looked amiss. His computer equipment hadn't been touched. But the closet door was open. A sound—soft humming—slowed his heart. She wasn't dead. But she was in his closet.

One slow step followed by another brought him to the closet door. His heart slammed into fourth as he surveyed the damage. He could barely take it all in. His suits had been squished together in a hodgepodge of styles and colors. His shoes were off the racks and piled haphazardly on the floor. Her things had taken over like a virus, killing the symmetry.

"What are you doing?" David would be proud. Charles's voice held none of his horror.

Her shoulders jerked with surprise as she spun around. Wide blue eyes met his. Her scarlet lips formed an O and her pale cheeks flushed pink. Then she smiled, not just with those lips but with her eyes. It was the oddest thing. "Charley," she whispered.

"Uh..."

"I know we have to get more hangers. We can do that tomorrow, okay? But for now, I think it's all right." She looked over her shoulder at the clothes she'd bought with his credit card.

He relaxed again. Not back to normal, but not three beats from a coronary, either.

"I have a few more things," she said, facing him again. "But for those I need a drawer."

This was going to kill him. No heart could race like this and not cause serious damage. Maybe he should take an aspirin. Or have a drink. Or both.

She took a step toward him and his plans for medication fled. Her face. He'd never seen it before. Not like this. It was a child's face in many ways—slightly rounded cheeks, skin so soft and pale that the closet light made her glow. But then there was that red lipstick, the slight, knowing smile. Those eyes that were equal parts mischief and innocence.

Another step brought her into his personal space. Close enough to see her eyes dilate. To smell roses. To understand what she meant to do.

He needed to distance himself from her. Step away. Get the hell out of there.

She touched his arm with delicate fingers. He swallowed, trying desperately to keep his cool. To not let her see that her touch had sent a jolt through him. It wasn't lightning, but it was real. And it had stirred him as surely as if her hand had landed much farther down his body.

"Charley," she whispered again, her voice oozing sex and sweetness. He'd hated the nickname since birth, but when she said it—

"You're all I've thought about for months. In every dream. In every shower. It's been you. Just...you."

It was time to leave. Time to run as fast as he could in any direction at all. But her fingers held him captive, her gaze made him stupid.

Her mouth, her moist scarlet lips, curved once more into the smile of a temptress. Those eyes...

Damn it. Damn it all to—

He gripped her arms with his hands, lifting her to his lips. Took her mouth with his own, stole her very breath.

Crazy. He was insane.

But a loaded pistol couldn't have stopped him. Hell, a whole army couldn't have stopped him.

5

HEAVEN. Heaven on earth in his arms. His hungry kiss, his hands gripping her with such reined-in passion meant she'd have bruises tomorrow. But she didn't mind. Not when it was Charley holding her like this. Charley, who fought so hard to stay aloof, to pretend he didn't care. She knew better. She'd always known better.

She opened her mouth and his tongue touched hers, a passionate blending so incredible her whole body trembled. The dance began, thrusting, tasting—mint and coffee. His scent was masculine. No artifice. No cologne at all. Just soap and the part of him that couldn't be washed away. The scent that made him undeniably Charley.

The only thing wrong was...she couldn't really move anything but her feet. He had her arms pressed against her body, her head stilled with his delicious mouth, and she was off the ground completely. She tried to touch the carpet with her right toe, but all she managed to do was sway a bit.

Then she got it. Oh, for heaven's sake! *He'd swept her off her feet.* Literally. Just as she'd always dreamed he would. Everything was going to be perfect. The wedding would go off without a hitch. The honeymoon—

Paris, maybe?—would set new records for stamina. And their life together? Bliss. Pure, sweet—

Charley's head reared back, and he looked at her as if he'd never seen her before. Her vision of a perfect future clicked off like a light switch. "Charley? What's wrong?"

"I—you—I—"

She smiled. "You silly goof. It's *me*. You don't have to pretend, Charley. I love you like this. With your armor down. Don't you know that by now?"

His mouth opened. Then shut.

"Uh, Charley?"

"What?"

"I'm starting to lose the feeling in my hands."

Again his mouth opened as he realized how he was holding her. He instantly lowered her and snatched his hands away so quickly his elbow hit the closet door frame with a loud crack.

She winced, knowing he'd hit his funny bone, which hurt like the dickens. He swore, a couple of good ones, and rubbed his injury.

"I'm seconds from being done here," she said, trying to shift his focus to something more pleasant. "Then we can make dinner. Together. Won't that be fun?"

He scowled. That bonk must have really hurt.

"How about something simple? Spaghetti. We can do that. Oh, it'll be lovely." She waggled her eyebrows. "And if you're very good, I'll show you some of the things I bought. The things from Victoria's Secret."

He paled. Visibly. And he got the most peculiar look on his face.

"Are you all right? Do we need a doctor?"

"One of us does."

"I'll call right away," she said as she headed toward the phone. He caught her by the arm. Mercy, but his touch did things to her. "What is it, darling?"

"I don't need a doctor."

"Are you sure? You might have fractured the bone."

"I didn't."

"All right. I won't call."

"Thank you."

"But..."

He sighed, still holding her in front of him. His look, this time, was enigmatic—half angry, half searching.

"You know what?"

"What?"

"I've been away too long, my love. Far too long. I feel terrible about it. If I'd known you were in this kind of shape—"

Those dark eyebrows of his came down ferociously. "What does that mean?"

"You're incredibly tense. You aren't breathing well. Your face is flushed. Need I go on? Charley, I mean this in the nicest possible way, but you look like hell."

He let go of her arm and used that hand to rub his temple. The brows didn't relax.

"Sweetie, I think you're stunning. But I know you at your peak. This isn't it."

"You're right. I'm not at my peak."

"You see? It's as if we'd never been apart." She walked to his bed and lifted the cover of the top box, tossing it to the floor behind her. She opened the tissue paper, and there it was: the most beautiful nightgown she'd ever seen. It was white, but very soft and very thin. There would be little left to his imagination, but that wasn't a minus at all. She lifted the exquisite garment from the box and held it in front of her.

Charley was right where she'd left him, and he seemed transfixed by the negligee. Of course, she knew he would be.

"You think I should wear this tonight?"

The sound that came out of him might have meant something, but to her ears, it was a slightly strangled grunt.

"Or this one?" She tossed the white nightgown on the bed and opened the second box. Oh, right. She'd gone a little nuts in that shop, but now she was glad for it.

She picked up the tiny red baby-doll pajamas and turned to show Charley.

His hand went to his neck, as if he was checking his pulse. Darn it, she knew he didn't look right. She'd talk to David about this. But not now. Not tonight.

The phone jangled and they both jumped. She was closest, so she picked it up. "Hello."

As a surprised woman's voice said "Hello?" back, Holly turned to see Charley lunge across the room, except he stepped on the box top, slid until he hit the wall, then sat down rather abruptly on the floor.

"Uh-oh. Are you all right?"

"I'm fine, dear," the woman said.

"Oops. I wasn't talking to you. Charley fell."

"Charley?"

"Yes. Charley Warren."

"I know who he is, dear. I gave birth to him."

"Oh!"

"The question is, who are you?"

Charley had gotten to his knees and grasped the edge of the bathroom door to haul himself up. He didn't seem to be hurt badly. She turned her attention to his mother. "I'm Holly."

"Holly? You don't...sound like Holly."

"I've been away. And matured, of course."

"Of course."

Holly sat down on the edge of the bed. She crossed her legs and leaned against the big headboard. "How are you?"

"Me? I'm fine. Just a little bewildered."

"Why?"

His mother cleared her throat. So that's where Charley had picked up the habit. "I must have had too much wine with dinner tonight."

"That's right, you're on the cruise. Is it wonderful?"

"Very. But I'm afraid I'm growing larger by the day. The food is simply too delicious to pass up, even though I tell myself I'm going to diet every day."

"I know exactly what you mean. I have that problem with pistachios. I can't resist them. I can't even stop myself from buying them. And then, after I swear I'll only have five a day, I look down and find a bag full of shells."

"That's it to a T."

"Is there something you like especially?"

His mother laughed, a light, high sound, more like a child's laugh than a woman of years. "Yes. I like the crème brûlée. It calls to me."

Holly looked up to find Charley standing in front of her. He wore a terrible scowl; his brows almost met in the middle. Her heart melted with regret that they'd been apart so long. He so clearly needed her.

"Charley wants to speak to you, but before I give him the phone, I just wanted to tell you how happy I am to have a chance to be in your family. I think we're going to get on famously. I hope you'll be back in time for the wedding."

Charley held out his hand, demanding the phone. It was a bit rude, actually.

"Wedding?" his mother asked.

"I think Charley wants to fill you in on the details. Bye now."

Holly didn't hear his mother reply. Charley grabbed the portable phone right out of her hand. Hmm. If ever a man needed a woman's touch... His manners were curt, he scowled much too much and she hadn't heard him laugh once. On the other hand, he sure could kiss.

Charley turned on his heel, stepped carefully over the box top and went into the bathroom, slamming the door behind him.

Holly didn't mind. It was good that he spoke to his mother. It said a great deal about his character. Besides, she had to find a drawer for her lingerie.

"NO, MOTHER, we're not getting married."

"But, Charley, she seems like such a sweet girl."

"Charles. My name is Charles. And she's not sweet, she's insane."

"Stop that. She isn't."

"No? Her name isn't Holly. It's Jane Dobson. Yesterday she was my personal assistant, which, before you even ask, is a glorified title for a gofer. I barely know her."

"Dobson? I just read a book by a Felicity Dobson."

"That's her sister."

"Honestly? Oh, I loved the book. It was wonderful. Such rich characterization. I think you should read it, Ch—"

"Mother!"

She sighed. "She just seems like such a sweet girl."

Charles leaned against the bathroom sink, hardly able to comprehend the unbelievably idiotic situation he was in. David had to be crazy to think he was going to put up with her. Lawsuit or no lawsuit, he was calling the police. And the men in the white coats.

"Charles?"

"Yes?"

"You aren't listening to me."

"Sorry, Mother. What?"

"I asked what on earth happened that she's calling herself Holly?"

"We don't know. Not for sure. An accident. She has a lump on her forehead, and her clothes were torn."

"Oh, Charles, you don't think... Is it possible the poor dear was molested?"

"Of course not," he said, but a second later he wasn't so sure. What if she had suffered something far more sinister than a conk on the head? What if—?

"Charles!"

"Yes, Mother?"

"I said, has she seen a doctor?"

"No."

"You call Sam right this minute. Well, as soon as we get off the phone. Have him do an examination."

"Yes, yes, of course. I will. Although David didn't think she was hurt badly."

"David isn't an internist, is he?"

"No. You're right. I'll take care of it."

"Good boy. And Charles? Be kind to her, would you? She sounds like a love. Like someone it would be good for you to know."

"I do know her. As an employee."

"That's not what I meant. You know who she reminds me of?"

"Your crazy aunt Lila?"

His mother cleared her throat with a specific intonation, one he was familiar with. He'd upset her. "She reminds me of me. When I first met your father."

"You thought you were someone else?"

"Charles. Please. I'm talking about the qualities of the girl that can't be manufactured by a bump on the head. She's got life in her. A true joie de vivre. I have such a strong feeling about her."

"A little too much joie, if you ask me."

"Hmm. I know that tone. You use it with me often enough. It was my joie that was so good for your father. We didn't have him for long, but while he was here, we had a time together. Such fun. And, sweetheart, believe me, when you reach the end of your days, you won't regret the times you didn't go to the office."

Fun? He'd never seen his father have fun. Not even on vacations. Well, there was that one time in the Hamptons. On the beach. He'd been shocked at his father's laughter, at the way he'd kissed his mother. A little embarrassed, too.

"Go find her, dear. And remember to be kind. You are, you know. Despite that terrible scowl of yours, you're one of the kindest people I've ever known. I'm very proud of you for that."

"Thank you," he said, although he didn't see how the compliment could apply to him. But then, it was Mother talking.

"I'll call tomorrow. I must know what's going to happen next."

"Fine. I'll speak to you then."

"Charles?"

"Yes?"

"I love you. You know that, don't you?"

"Of course. And I love you."

"Good."

She clicked off, and he pushed the button on his phone to hang up. When he got the dial tone, he called David's cell phone and paced the small room impatiently.

"Levinson."

"David. What if she's been molested? If that's why she's—"

"Whoa, whoa. Calm down. She hasn't been."

"How do you know? You're not an internist."

"Despite that, I'm still capable of picking up a telephone. I spoke to the doctor who took care of her."

"Well?"

"Give me a minute, for God's sake, I'm cooking."

"Cook later. Tell me."

"I don't know what she sees in you."

"David."

"She was hit in the head by a plaster Cupid."

"By a *what*?"

"A plaster Cupid. It fell from the ledge of a building. Not just any building, mind you. Your building."

"Damn."

"I concur. However, the good news is, they did an MRI, and there's no swelling, no permanent damage at all."

"So what's with the Holly business?"

"It's temporary. It's going to fade in short order. But until it does, and of its own accord, it's important that you play along."

"I can't."

"Why not?"

Charles sat down on the edge of the tub. "She bought a nightgown."

"And?"

"A see-through nightgown."

"Ah, I'm beginning to see the light here."

"David, she's my employee. It's not appropriate for her to be here wearing...that."

"Right."

Was that a muffled chuckle? Was David actually laughing about this? "This isn't funny. Not in the least. She told my mother we're getting married. She wants to cook spaghetti!"

"For God's sake, Charles, get a grip. You've negotiated with Trump and won hands down. How hard can it be to placate one young woman for one night?"

"Trump never came to the table in a see-through nightie."

"You're a big boy, Charles. You can do this. Now, I'm going to get my dinner before it's burned. Have a nice night."

Charles told him where he could put his dinner, but David hung up before he got to the good part. Have a nice night. Right.

He'd kissed her. Not the other way around. *He'd* kissed *her*. What did that say about his character? About his fortitude? The only solution was to set her up in the guest room immediately, then lock himself in his room. He didn't dare talk with her, and heaven forbid she should make good on her threat to show him more of her lingerie purchases.

It was a hell of a position to be in. How does a plaster Cupid come to fall on a person's head? And why did it have to be his building? Just his luck, huh?

He got up, went to the sink, splashed some cold water on his face. He wasn't going to get involved with her. All that was necessary was to carry out his plan: let her talk, just don't listen. It would work. It would.

After drying his face and running a hand through his hair, he opened the bathroom door.

Holly—Jane—stood in front of him, except she was wearing the little red baby dolls. He hadn't been certain about them being see-through before. He was now.

6

HOLLY LIFTED HER right brow, the perfect punctuation to the slinky red outfit she had slipped into while Charley was in the bathroom. She'd positioned herself against the closet door frame, her hands provocatively behind her, flat on the door and wall. Her left foot was raised, also flat on the door. She was a vamp, a temptress, Rita Hayworth, Marilyn Monroe.

The effect of her outfit and her pose was right on the money. One more second and his jaw would drop to the floor. The brazen move wasn't something she felt one hundred percent comfortable with, but that was okay. This time, she was going to be brave. She was going to be sexy as sin. She was going to drive him wild.

"What—"

She smiled seductively as Charley's voice cracked on the single word. "Do you like it?"

He cleared his throat. Twice. "It's very, uh, very attractive."

"Is that all? Attractive?"

He shook his head as his gaze traveled down her body. She flushed as he lingered on her breasts. The material was so transparent, he could see her nipples. They, if nothing else, should give him a strong indication of her intentions. He finished his lazy perusal at the tip of her toes, her red high heels turning his pale cheeks pink. Then he moved his gaze up again, but he never reached her face.

She realized he wasn't going to do anything except stare, so she would have to take the initiative. She was Lauren Bacall, Jessica Rabbit. She headed straight for him, wiggling her behind like a stripper about to take it all off.

"What are you doing?"

"You're all the way over there," she whispered, trying to get just the right breathy quality. "And I'm all the way over here."

"Don't."

"Don't?"

"You don't have to come any closer. I can see you just fine."

"But you can't touch."

"I don't want to touch."

She knew that wasn't true. Everything about him told her exactly what he wanted to do. And touch was just the beginning.

"Charley, you don't have to be shy with me."

"I am. I'm terribly shy. So why don't you get dressed and we'll meet in the kitchen."

"Nice try, mister. I hear 'no, no' on your lips, but I see 'yes, yes' in your eyes."

"My eyes are liars."

Three steps away from him, she stopped, then rolled her right shoulder in a slow circle. "I don't think so, Charley."

She lifted her opposite hand to her strap and pushed the thin material to her arm. She was Gypsy Rose Lee, Madonna.

"What are you doing?"

Oh, what turmoil he was in. She could see it every-where—his dark hair furrowed by his fingers, his brows doing their best to meet, his cheeks trying to de-cide whether to pale or go crimson. He was a mess, the man who was whispered about in financial circles, who dismissed secretaries as frequently as he changed his socks. This man, the man who had been the center of her dreams and hopes and wishes for longer than she could remember, was a bumbling, stumbling fool who couldn't keep his eyes off her.

There should be a way to capture this moment and press it into a scrapbook. To save and savor the way he struggled so hard to keep his gaze from her chest. What power. What delicious power.

She moved closer and caressed his cheek with her palm. His warmth seeped into her instantly. His scratchy five o'clock shadow was both intimate and ex-citing. "Charley, why don't you admit it? You want this as much as I do."

"I don't."

"You don't find me attractive?"

His mouth fell open for a few seconds. "You're jok-ing, right? You're incredible."

The game stopped. Hot tears blurred her vision, and her chest felt tight with pressure. Darkness crept up be-hind her, and for a moment she felt sure she was going to faint.

His hand was on her arm. "Holly? What is it?"

She shook her head, unable to speak. Not with the lump in her throat. She turned from him only to face herself in his mirror.

What was going on? Why did she seem so unfamiliar? My God, she was practically naked! How had she got—

"Holly?"

Relief swept through her, taking the strange little fugue state with it. She felt him behind her and she sagged against him. He held her, tentatively at first, but then she felt the pressure of his fingers on her arms. Gently, he pushed her forward and turned her around. "Are you all right?"

She nodded. "I don't know what that was about. But it doesn't matter. I think I'm just hungry."

"Get changed, then, and we'll go out for dinner."

"You don't want to make it here? With me?"

He searched her eyes for a long minute. "All right. But only if you put on something decent."

She frowned with what she was sure was a beguiling pout. "It's been so long, Charley. I thought—"

"I know. I've thought about it, too. The thing is, I assumed we were going to wait."

"Till bedtime?"

"Till the wedding."

"Oh. My. Why that's…that's so…sweet."

He sighed as he smiled. "I'm glad you don't think I'm being too old-fashioned."

"No, no. It's fine. Honestly. It's rather charming."

"Good. But I won't be able to resist you if you dress like that."

"Hmm. Should I make it hard on you, Charley?"

His smile disappeared. "You have. Believe me."

She laughed. "I didn't mean it that way, but I'll still take that as a compliment."

"Just, please, go change. I'm begging."

"I will. But just because I love you."

"Thank you."

She waggled one finger in front of his face. "Uh, uh, uh. No changing without a proper thank-you."

His clever dark eyes grew confused again. Which was just how she liked them.

"A proper thank-you is done not with words. Although the lips are definitely involved."

"Oh, no."

She nodded.

He looked at the door, then at the bed, then at her breasts.

He kissed her.

He tried to make it a small kiss, a peck. But her hand was too fast moving to the back of his neck. School was in session, and she was about to teach him how to say an appropriate *merci.*

He learned very quickly.

TWO SECONDS LONGER and he would have given in. As it was, he'd left her too abruptly, tearing himself away from the cool hand on his neck, and her warm lips. Closing his eyes hadn't helped. The image of her sweet young body in that—that slip of gauzy nothing had turned his brain to mush.

It was outrageously inappropriate for him to have seen her like that. But, to his utter horror, that was a large part of his desire for her. It was insane, and he didn't just mean her thinking she was Holly. The way he wanted her had him completely flummoxed.

He crossed the living room, straight to the bar. He

concentrated on making himself a dry martini, held himself back from simply tilting the gin bottle into his mouth. It didn't seem to matter that his bedroom door was closed. Her body lingered in his mind's eye, like that terrible white dot after being caught by a flash-bulb. He couldn't shake her, and he couldn't stop his own physical reaction.

There had been a time in his life when sex and women were on his mind constantly. In college it had been hard to concentrate on his studies, hard to get to sleep at night. He'd walked around in a semi-aroused state from morning till night, and there had been no cure for it. Except, of course, when he was actually with a woman.

Holly had been that woman for him. The real Holly. Ironically, Jane, who couldn't remember her own name, had stirred up some long-forgotten memories from his past. Holly had been his first. She'd made him wait for a full six months before she'd finally let him in her bed. And then it had been fantastic, but too fast. She'd never encouraged him to slow down, either. She was, however, big on talking afterward. Mostly about her social life. About her friends, and their friends, and who they all knew.

After Holly, who'd been the only one all during col-lege, there had been two others. Both of them women he'd met through friends of his mother's. Both of them had been nice enough, but the sex? It had been merely a release, and for that he'd been grateful.

Then his father had died and Charles's social life had come to a screeching halt. David kept trying to set him up, and sometimes he succeeded. But only for dinner and a concert, or a party. Charles had never taken the women home. Not when he'd have to be up so early for the Asian market.

The responsibility of the business had taken precedence. But he'd realized it wasn't advantageous to be single for too long. And Holly had seemed right.

Only now, he wasn't so sure.

His feelings for Jane were totally unlike anything he'd felt before. She unleashed something wild in him, and frankly, it scared him to death.

He wanted to ravish her. Throw her onto the bed, rip her clothes off, take her like a caveman.

The Tanqueray gin still had the cap on it. He remedied that situation, poured the liquor into his shaker, added a soupçon of vermouth, crushed ice, and then shook the mother until his arms got tired. Then he got his martini glass out of the freezer and poured the drink almost to the rim, leaving room for two olives.

His hand was none too steady as he brought the icy drink to his lips. But it certainly went down smoothly.

The couch was next, and he sagged into it like an old man. The rich leather failed to comfort him; even the view of Manhattan didn't give him any pleasure. Only this morning his life had been orderly, his biggest worry the Riverside deal. Now, Riverside and his pasty attorney could go jump in the Hudson, for all Charles cared. He was trapped in some devilish nightmare, a wet dream from which he couldn't awaken.

The bedroom door opened, but he didn't look up. Not at first. What would she be in this time? A teddy? One of his shirts? Absolutely nothing?

"What are you drinking?"

God, even her voice confused him—childlike and sensual mixed together in a wicked brew. He took a large sip of the biting drink and looked at her. Thank God. She'd changed into jeans and a sweater. Of course, the jeans fit low on her hips, and the sweater didn't quite reach her waist. The tantalizing strip of flesh was just enough to torture him.

She'd put on fresh lipstick and done something to her hair. The blond curls swayed as she walked, and so did her hips. Everything about her was womanly, and yet her eyes were young and full of mischief, her skin as delicate as a porcelain doll. She confused him in ways he'd never been confused before. He knew she was in her mid-twenties, and yet there was something forbidden in her youthful looks. He also knew that she wasn't doing this to him on purpose, but that didn't assuage his feelings of being ambushed.

"Hello?" she said as she reached the couch. "Earth to Charley. Are you there?"

"Yes. What?"

"I asked what you were drinking."

"A martini."

She wrinkled her nose, and he had to stop himself from grabbing her arm and pulling her down beside him. "I don't like martinis. What else do you have?"

He nodded to the bar. "Knock yourself out."

"Thanks." Her smile dazzled him as she sashayed in front of him.

Surely she must know what that walk suggested. Even with amnesia, she couldn't be that naive. On the contrary. Her seduction was too seamless to be unrehearsed, too casual to be anything less than a diabolical plot to drive him over the edge.

"Is it amaretto and cream that's a toasted almond?"

He shuddered. "I have no earthly idea. It sounds more like candy than a drink."

"It's good. You should try it. Sort of a milk shake with a kick."

"I don't like milk shakes."

She looked at him over her shoulder. "Just when, exactly, did you have your last milk shake?"

"I don't know. When I was a child."

"Aha! Then you don't know if you like milk shakes or not."

"Of course I do."

She shook her head as she poured a good jigger of amaretto into a Waterford crystal glass. Not finding any cream in his bar fridge, she headed for the kitchen.

It was impossible not to stare at her behind. It wasn't big; in fact, she was very slender everywhere. But the way she fit in the faded denim, her derriere a perfect heart, and the way her hips curved and swayed, he had to take another drink just to keep from moaning.

She opened the refrigerator, and he lost sight of her. It was then he noticed his pulse, his dry mouth even while drinking, his slightly damp palms.

Damn it, he wasn't some sex-crazed teenager. He ran a business empire. A tight ship. A winning team. He'd heard how people talked about him. They said he didn't have feelings. That his veins were filled with fiber optics, not blood. The secretarial pool called him Iron Charley, although never to his face.

And this sad creature who'd been conked on the

head was turning him into a whimpering, simpering fool.

"Got it," she said, bringing the carton of cream back to the bar with her. "After drinks, we'll make dinner, okay? I'm really hungry."

"Yes. All right."

She finished pouring her sweet concoction, stirred a little too vigorously for the delicate crystal, then carried her drink to the couch. He prayed she wouldn't sit close, but she did. Too close. Her hip touched him. Her elbow and her shoulder, too. Her scent slipped inside him, and the picture of her in that damn nightie threatened to do him in.

"Umm. This is so good. You have to try it."

He realized she was holding the silly drink under his nose. Even the smell was sickeningly sweet. "It's really not my cup of tea."

"How do you know unless you try?"

"I don't like dessert wine, so why would I like this?"

She took the drink away, but pouted as she did so. "Do you like custard?"

"Occasionally."

"How about almonds?"

"Yes. I like almonds."

She raised the drink under his nose again. "Then you'll like this."

He closed his eyes. "Fine. I'll taste the damn drink."

"Sip," she whispered.

His eyes shot open to find her tipping the glass, feeding him like a child! It was unthinkable. And yet he sipped. It was god-awful. Like liquid sugar. Not even close to a proper drink.

"Oh. Well, at least you tried. That's something."

"But I knew I wouldn't like it."

"I didn't like cucumbers."

"Pardon?"

"I said, I didn't like cucumbers when I was a kid. Couldn't stand the things. But I wanted to like them because they were very low in calories and so good for me. So every couple of years I'd give them a try. Honestly, the taste just set me shuddering. Like you just did. But then, last year I tried one, and you know what?"

"You liked it."

"No. It was terrible. But I realized there was no reason to stop trying them because, who knows, one day I just might like them."

He stared at her. No words came to him at all. He was, perhaps for the first time, utterly speechless. He had the feeling it wouldn't be the last time. Not if she was near.

She took another sip of her drink, and when she lowered the glass, a slim mustache of amaretto and cream lined her upper lip. "So, are we ready to start cooking?"

He brushed his upper lip, with no results. Then he nodded at her with his chin. "You've got...you know."

"What?"

"On your lip."

She touched the lower lip.

"No, not that one. The other one. A mustache."

"Really? Where?"

He pointed. "There. On your upper lip."

Her head moved slowly from side to side, although her gaze held steady.

He understood. Finally. It wouldn't do him any good to protest. And she was just peculiar enough to leave it there all night. Yet another form of torture. So he gave in. His cocked brow let her know he wasn't amused, but he brought his fingertips to her lip.

She pulled away, not letting him touch her. "That's not the right way," she said, her voice as husky as a whiskey sour.

"What are you talking— Oh, no."

She put her drink down on the coffee table, then faced him dead-on.

"No. Absolutely no."

She smiled, looking absurd with the milk there on her face. "How do you know you don't like something if you don't try it?"

"I've tried it, remember?"

"Yes. And I also remember you seemed to like it a lot."

"Why are you doing this to me?"

Her hand went to his thigh, and he jumped at the contact. Thankfully, he'd had enough of his martini that it didn't spill.

"I'm doing this, Charley, because I can."

"You are a devil."

She nodded. "Let me show you what I want," she whispered. Before he could stop her, she'd leaned over him until her warm breath caressed his face, then she slowly licked his upper lip from one end to the other.

The martini glass fell to the Persian carpet. He didn't give a damn.

7

HOLLY TOOK HER TIME, lapping his lip like a mother cat. The raspy nubs of his late-day beard tickled in a sexy sort of way. As soon as she'd reached the corner of his mouth, she headed back, moving her tongue down a bit. Tasting his martini. It wasn't bad this way. Slightly bitter, cool, and of course it helped that she tasted Charley, too. She licked his bottom lip, and his moan started low and deep. She didn't get another lick in. His hands stilled her, and then he pushed her back as if to bolt, but instead he kissed her. Kissed her as if he meant to steal her very soul. Opening his mouth, tasting her, thrusting, sucking, licking...no move too intimate, no line that wasn't crossed.

She'd never been kissed like this before; no woman ever had. He possessed her completely, played her like a violin, and when his hand went to her breast, she arched her back for more. The heat through the material made her squirm. As he found her nipple and squeezed it gently, she cried out. But his lips quieted her. The only thing she could do was kiss him back. And touch him. She found his belt and worked her hand down until she felt his hardness. So thick, so big...straining against his zipper so hard it would have to give.

This want, this excitement flowing through her veins

was unlike anything she'd ever felt. Her dreams had never been up to the task; she knew that now. She wanted him with her whole body, her whole spirit. It was a need, not a wish. She was unfinished without him.

He pulsed beneath her hand. There was only one place they could go from here. If they did, it would be her fault. She didn't want to start their marriage that way. Despite her want, her need, she lifted her hand and pulled away from his kisses. He looked at her with dazed eyes. Pleading eyes.

She stood, then headed for the kitchen on rubbery legs. She had to snap out of it. Both of them did. "I'm going to put on a pot of coffee," she said, forcing her voice to sound bright and shiny as if she hadn't just been kissed to the moon and back. "You know, I don't mind some of those jars of sauce. They can be pretty good. Especially Newman's Own spaghetti sauce. Have you tried that? Of course, homemade is better, but that takes ages, and I'm simply starving. Is a salad all right?"

She opened the fridge door, welcoming the shock of cold air. "Let's see what you have in the crisper."

Charles suppressed a moan. He wondered if there were hidden cameras around, if this was some sort of sick joke. Probably not. He wasn't that lucky.

She was for real, and he couldn't keep his hands off her.

"Balsamic is my favorite. I love it. I don't even need oil with it, just that aged sweet vinegar."

What in hell was she babbling about? As if that made a difference. She could be speaking Norwegian for all his libido cared. The thing was, he'd always prided himself on his attitude toward women. He'd never been the kind of man to go out with a beautiful woman just because she'd look good on his arm. But the way his thoughts had spun all evening, he felt like Joe Neanderthal. The only thing missing was his club.

She reached up to get a glass, revealing several more inches of her stomach, and he had to close his eyes. He wanted her. He wanted to do everything to her, with her, from the missionary position to the entire *Kama Sutra*.

"Aren't you going to help?"

He opened his eyes. She wasn't reaching for anything, so he felt a little more secure about joining her in the kitchen. But first he picked up his glass, went to the bar and poured himself another martini. One sip was all he needed.

She smiled at him, showing off those even white teeth.

He tossed the rest of the drink back, shuddered as it went down, then squared his shoulders, determined to be the perfect gentleman.

But as he took his first step, the temptation to run to his bedroom was strong. Very strong. He could lock the door. Stay there until she came out of this thing, or he starved to death. That would work.

"Charley?"

"Yes?"

"Come on. The water's almost boiling and you haven't even started the salad."

He went into the kitchen. But it didn't feel like his kitchen. It was much too small. Even though she was at the stove and he stood in front of the island, he could still smell her perfume. Still feel her heat.

"I've put out everything. You can start with the lettuce."

Before him was an array of salad ingredients, from iceberg lettuce and arugula to baby carrots and marinated artichoke hearts. A large wooden bowl was to the right of the chopping board, upon which lay a Henckels chef's knife.

After washing his hands in the island sink, he started tearing up the lettuce, but every few seconds he looked over his shoulder to watch her. All she was doing was stirring the spaghetti, and yet...

He was drawn to her. Physically, of course, but something else was going on. In her own weird way, she'd gotten to the part of him he'd shut down. Not purposely. It hadn't been a conscious decision. But now that it was back, he realized just how long it had been gone.

He'd read a statistic somewhere that men think about sex around eighty-six times a day. He was making up for long days, months, weeks where his mind had been focused on work and nothing else.

"Charley?"

"Yes?"

"Are you planning on inviting guests?"

"Pardon?"

She glanced at the bowl. He followed her gaze and saw that he'd broken up the entire head of lettuce. "I was going to leave some for us and put the rest in the fridge. For tomorrow. In case we wanted another salad."

"Uh-huh."

He cleared his throat and concentrated on cutting the tomatoes.

"I liked talking to your mother."

"She liked talking to you." Too much.

"Where is she?"

"In the Caribbean. Somewhere around Saint Thomas."

"Oh, I'd like to go there. Does she go on a lot of cruises?"

"Every one she can."

"Really? Where's the colander?"

He looked at the cupboard next to her, but that didn't seem right. Then at the cupboard by the microwave. "I don't know."

She started looking, opening and closing cupboard doors. "Not much of a cook, eh?"

"I have someone who cooks for me most days. And if she's not here, I go out."

"No kidding? I think I'd really miss cooking."

"I was never that fond of it to begin with."

"Eureka! I have found it!" She straightened triumphantly with the plastic colander held high.

"Good for you."

Her dazzling smile took his breath for a minute, and he almost sliced his thumb. His attention went back to his task.

"Does she have special friends who go with her?"

"Who?"

"Your mother."

"No. She goes by herself. And I send a couple of people to look out for her."

"Paid people?"

"Yes."

"Doesn't she have any friends?"

"She makes plenty of friends on board. She's the life of the party wherever she is."

"I don't understand. Why are you paying people to look after her?"

His sigh came out louder than he'd intended. "My mother is eccentric."

"Which isn't a crime, is it?"

"Nope."

"So what makes her so eccentric?"

"Well, there was one time in Alaska when she bought a fifty-foot totem pole and had it sent to my office."

Holly laughed. The sound rippled through him, forcing him to look at her again. She had oven mitts on, and she was carrying the steaming pot to the sink. He stopped himself from going to her, from taking the pot right out of her hands. She wasn't a child. Surely she'd poured hot water before without mishap.

"What happened to it?"

"The totem pole?"

"Uh-huh."

"I donated it to the Metropolitan Museum."

"That was nice of you. But it was nice of her, too. I'm sure she thought you'd like it."

"I did. Although it cost me almost a hundred thousand dollars by the time it was safely at the museum."

"Wow. That's a lot of money."

"It is indeed."

"So what else? What other eccentric things has Mother done?"

He ripped open the bag of baby carrots. "She got lost in Crete for three days. We found her in a nudist colony, where she'd bought a three-year membership."

"You've got to admit, she has style."

"Oh, yes."

He heard the distinct slosh of pasta being tossed, water draining from the small holes down the drain. Then the plop when it landed in the ceramic bowl. Suddenly, he was hungry. For food.

"Have you ever gone with her?"

"Me?"

"Yes."

"No."

"Why not?"

"The cruises last for weeks. I don't have that kind of time."

"Oh, that's a shame. I think she'd love it."

"She does very well on her own." He turned to find her staring at him. "Cucumbers?"

"Pardon?"

"You brought them out, but I wasn't sure you wanted them in the salad."

"I do. It's time I tried them again."

"Fine by me."

He didn't turn away until she did. Then he got busy, kept his hands and his mind occupied.

"Charley?"

He couldn't help it. He smiled. "Yes?"

"What made you put the ad in the magazine? I

mean, I know you wanted to find me, but why now? Why me?"

"I didn't want—" Damn it. He'd almost said too much. He cleared his throat while he sought an acceptable answer. "I didn't want to lose any more time. I've always regretted that we lost touch. But for all I knew, you'd gotten married and had five children."

A gentle touch on his elbow stilled his hands.

"I wouldn't. I waited for you. I would have waited forever."

Dropping the knife, he turned. Her cheeks were infused with pink, but her gaze was straightforward. She didn't shrink from his perusal one iota. "Why?" he murmured.

"Because I love you."

"Do you?"

She nodded. "More than anything. Or anyone. I've always loved you."

"Are you sure?"

"Of course. Charley, can't you feel it? Every time I look at you I tremble inside. When you touch me, I barely know my own name. I get all fuzzy and confused. When I touch you, I think all sorts of things. Wicked things."

"You do?"

She nodded. "This is fate, my darling Charley. With a capital *F*."

"It's...something. I'll grant you that."

"You know, for the guy who instigated this whole business, you sure are cautious."

"Well, I guess I have some of my very own eccentricities."

She took in a deep breath, then let it out slowly. "You do. And so do I. It's what makes us wonderful, don't you think?"

"No, I don't."

"I think that's why I'm here. To help change your mind." With that little comment, she turned on her heel and went back to the stove to check on the bubbling sauce.

He made an executive decision about the salad—it didn't need another thing. As he put the remaining vegetables in plastic, he pondered asking her some pointed questions. Maybe that's all she needed to be nudged back into her own life. Nothing shocking, like saying her name or anything, but a gentle hint or two?

He'd wait until they were sitting down. He put the extra vegetables in the crisper, including the lettuce, while she whipped up a balsamic vinaigrette, using Dijon mustard, freshly ground pepper, with a final drizzle of extra virgin olive oil. When she was finished, he put the salad on the table, then helped Holly find the silverware and plates. She brought the pasta while he got out the pitcher of ice water.

He continued to wait as they served each other, as he tasted his salad, the pasta. He watched, fascinated, at the way she separated her food on the plate. A dollop of pasta at the twelve o'clock position. A tablespoon of sauce at three o'clock. Six pieces of lettuce at six o'clock and one slice of cucumber at nine.

When she finished, she smiled so contentedly he didn't have the heart to ask her what in the hell she was doing. He just ate for a while, hardly tasting the food as he struggled with what question to ask her.

Finally, after she'd eaten all the way around her plate, right up to the cucumber, he made his decision. But first, he wanted to see what she was going to do now.

With knife and fork firmly in hand, she sliced the cucumber into four equal wedges. Then she put the knife down and speared a piece with her fork. But she didn't eat it yet. She looked at it for a long moment, then dipped the morsel into the remaining drops of vinaigrette on her plate. When she was satisfied, she aimed the fork at her mouth, her hand inching its way up and up until she popped it in her mouth. She chewed, smiling triumphantly. But the victory was short-lived. He watched her beautiful face scrunch up into a perfect mask of distaste. But she did finish chewing, and she swallowed every bit.

"No good, huh?"

She shook her head. "Maybe next year."

"Maybe. Can I serve you some more pasta?"

"I'll get it. Thanks."

"Um, Holly. I was just wondering. About your mother."

Her hand froze midreach. A few seconds ticked by, then she got the pasta bowl and lifted it to the side of her plate. "What about my mother?"

"I don't know what's going on with her. You haven't said anything."

Her brows came down, and so did the corners of her lips. The vivacious creature that had tempted him all night shrank before his very eyes. It was as if someone had opened a drain, and the life was seeping out of her second by second. He wanted to shoot himself for opening his big mouth. Obviously she wasn't ready for such a blatant question.

"She's...she's..."

"Is she still living in Paris?"

"Yes! Paris."

"I'm glad. She likes it there so much. Would you pass me the salad, please?"

She did. And slowly, the color returned to her cheeks. But he felt awful, and a little worried now about what was okay to say and what wasn't. But he had to try again. Change the subject to something safe. "This was very good pasta. Thank you."

"Thank me? It was the salad that made the dinner."

"You're just saying that."

"No. Honestly. It's wonderful." She put another small piece of lettuce into her mouth.

He didn't understand about the food. Or about what was happening to her. He just was happy Holly was back. But Holly wasn't back at all, was she?

He needed a good night's sleep. By tomorrow, this should be over, and he could go back to his regularly scheduled life. It was already eight. He'd wash the dishes, then set her up in the guest room. Suggest she take a long, hot bath.

Then he'd lock himself inside his room and pray he had the wherewithal to get some work done.

What was the deal with her food?

SHE DRIED THE LAST DISH and handed it to Charley. He put it on the stack of the other matching dishes, white with a single gold band around the edge. They were stunning, but then all his things were stunning. The kitchen was practically a work of art. The streamlined island, the recessed lighting, that silver refrigerator flush with the cabinetry. All of it coordinated in granite colors. Masculine, efficient and beautiful. Just like Charley.

He nodded toward the living room, and she took a moment to see that, too. Of course she'd noticed the large leather couch. Not ordinary leather. This was finer than that. Kidskin—that's what they called it. The deep sienna was repeated in the club chair and echoed in the abstract painting over the fireplace. Everything in the room went with everything else in the room, right down to the fresh flowers on the end table. But there was something a little unsettling about such unmitigated perfection. It was as if this was a model for a home, not a home.

The place needed a woman's touch. Not just a housekeeper. Once they were married, Holly would find the humanity in the room, starting with the details. There weren't any knickknacks anywhere. No odd piece of pottery picked up at a sidewalk art festival. No pictures on the mantelpiece.

"Can I get you a drink?"

She shook her head. "I have a little headache."

"Want some aspirin?"

"Yes, please."

He headed for his room, and she went to the only place in the living room that showed any real life. His bookshelves. There were a great many classics, from Shakespeare to Dickens. But there were also more interesting choices. An entire set of books by C. S. Forester, all about Horatio Hornblower. Next to that he'd compiled all of Michael Crichton's books. And Tom Clancy, too. She pulled one out, Forester's *Hornblower and the Hotspur*. It was well-read, with some dog-eared pages, a few scribbled notes in the margins. The binding was a little wobbly, too.

It made her like the room. And it made her love Charley all the more. He did have dreams. He'd traveled in his imagination, and the journey there never stopped with the printed word.

She wanted to know his dreams, and more than that she wanted to help make his dreams come true. After all, that's what he'd done for her. It was only fair.

A footfall heralded his return from the bedroom. "I brought you two aspirin. Is that all right?"

"It's perfect," she said. "Just perfect."

8

SHE TOOK ONE PILL at a time. Charley watched, fascinated, as she placed the first caplet on the middle of her tongue, sipped a bit of water, then threw her head back in a swallow that would have suggested taking a week's worth of vitamins. The second pill went down the same way. She then finished off the water and held out the glass. "Thank you."

"You're welcome."

"I was looking at your books."

"Oh?"

"I love that you love to read."

"I'm glad I could make you happy."

After gifting him with a slow smile, she ran her fingers across his *Story of Civilization* set. "What else do you love, Charley?"

"You don't know?"

She shook her head. "I have my suspicions, but I'd like to hear it from you."

The inquiry was serious, given the low pitch of her voice. Which undoubtedly meant the conversation was going to be lengthy. His *Wall Street Journal* waited, still folded, in his briefcase. The CNBC financial news had already started. The itch to say no to her, to go to his room and do what he did night after night after night, was strong.

Instead, he walked to the couch and sat down. "So what was the question again?"

She didn't answer immediately, but joined him. To his relief, she chose the opposite end of the sofa. As with taking her pills, she made something of a production of the simple act. First, she curled her right leg on the cushion, then sat on her leg and scooted back. But that wasn't all. The free leg came up on the couch, too, and her delicate fingers linked together over her shin. He'd have hurt himself if he tried that, but she looked contented as a kitten.

"I want to know what you love," she said finally.

"That's not an easy question."

"It should be."

"Tell you what. You go first. Give me a chance to consider this."

She nodded, her expression thoughtful. Beautiful. Now he wasn't so certain he wanted her all the way over there.

"I love the sunrise. Getting up very early, when it's still dark, and going to the top of the highest building I can find, then watching the sun wake up Manhattan."

"Go on."

"I love Sondheim musicals."

"Oh, well, who doesn't?"

She gave a fetching pout. "You're making fun."

"Yeah, I am. But don't worry. I like him, too."

"Just for that, it's your turn."

"Only two? I thought you'd go on for hours."

"Don't change the subject."

He stared at the wall, at his favorite painting. The limited edition had cost a small fortune, even though the artist was just starting to develop a name. But it was worth it. There was something about the shadows. The way the hat brim hid most of the central figure's face, but not his expression. The details of the bustling street were vibrant. The other people—the women, the businessmen, the traffic cop—all looked as if they had somewhere to go. As if they belonged there. But not the man in the hat. He was quite still, his hands in his pockets, his hat brim pulled down.

"You love that painting?"

He nodded. "I've never really thought about it that way—loving it. But I like it a great deal."

"Why?"

"Why does anyone like art? It speaks to me."

She turned her head slightly to the right to ponder the canvas. "It's lonely, don't you think?"

"No. I think it's about solitude. About standing on your own two feet. That's different."

She sighed, and he wondered if it was Holly's sigh or Jane's.

"I think he's lonely. Terribly lonely. The way he hides, the way he doesn't look at anything... It's like he's standing in the middle of the ocean, when the waves are tossing and turning everything around him, but he never gets wet."

"Maybe he doesn't want to get wet."

She looked at Charles, her gaze as passionate as it had been in his bedroom closet. "No one wants to be on the outside."

He thought about arguing the point, then changed his mind. "You're right. No one does."

She nodded, but he didn't think the gesture was

meant for him. Her gaze had wandered. She wasn't looking at the painting, or anything else for that matter.

"I know it's not very late, but would you mind if I went to bed now?"

"No," he said, way too quickly, before he considered what was behind the abrupt change of plan. "I mean, uh, not at all. You've had a difficult day."

"Yeah. Very difficult."

She uncurled herself as he stood up, and they headed for the back of the penthouse. She veered off at the bathroom while he went on to the guest room.

He flipped on the light and was taken aback at the drab colors. He hadn't been in here for a long time, but his memory wasn't of these dark grays and dull burgundys. The comforter's design was of geometric shapes. The lamp was ultramodern halogen, the small desk and chair totally bereft of anything but function.

She didn't belong in this room. But there wasn't much choice. He turned down the corner of the comforter in an effort to make things seem cozier, but all it did was add another geometric shape.

Shaking his head, he left the room, passing the closed door to the bathroom on his way to the living room. There, he got the vase of fresh flowers. That would help. A lot.

While Holly prepared for bed, he moved several of her boxes to the floor of the guest closet. No need to take any of the hanging clothes. They wouldn't be in his closet long enough to be a nuisance.

He made one more trip across the apartment, this time to fetch a small carafe of filtered water and a glass. She might get thirsty in the middle of the night.

Although his mother, and even David, would congratulate him on his consideration for Holly, Charles realized by the time he'd finished fussing that he'd made a tactical error. A big one.

All this preparation for bed had got him thinking about...bed. It wasn't exactly a leap. The sheets weren't very inventive, just plain gray, but they were soft. As he plumped the pillow, he thought of Holly's skin, about the softness of her breasts, the way her curves were built for his hands—

Oh, damn it. He was off to the races. And he hadn't even seen which pajamas she was going to wear.

The smart thing to do was go to his room, shut the door and lock it. The end. If he had to take a sleeping pill, so be it. But work would probably do the trick. He had a lot to catch up on, so why in hell was he standing here like a French maid waiting for the mistress?

Oh, great. Now he was thinking of Holly as his mistress while she was dressed like a French maid! Did cold showers really work?

He hustled himself out of her room and down the hall. He didn't even stop to say good-night to her. The light was on in the guest room and she was a clever girl. She'd figure out where she was going to sleep for the night.

He shut the door to his own bedroom and turned the lock. Relaxing his shoulders, he breathed in and out like a normal human. All he had to do was get through the night. That's what David said. Good man, that David.

Charles got his pajamas out of his drawer, then went into his bathroom to change and get ready for bed. He took a little more time than usual, but at least he had his answer: cold water did work. If it was applied to the right area. However, the effect was brief. One would, he imagined, have to stand in a freezing river for a considerable time to cool one's body from someone as tempting as Holly.

Finally, he was ready for bed. Work would have to wait, as his mind was officially mush. He turned off the bathroom light, then the lamp over his chair, pushed one of Holly's boxes aside and slipped between his own sheets.

Visions of baby-doll pajamas danced in his head, and he wasn't happy about it. For God's sake, he hadn't even opened the *Journal*. He hadn't looked at NASDAQ or the Dow, or anything. She'd completely disrupted his whole day, and his whole night.

The only thing stopping him from tossing the troublemaker out on her ear was his own sense of honor. Of responsibility. David had been right. If Jane had been his mother, he'd want someone to take care of her like this. He'd be downright grateful.

Go to sleep.

Right.

His mind raced a mile a minute, every thought starring one Jane Dobson, aka Holly Baskin. Holly! It hadn't even occurred to him. Had she seen the ad? What if she called, and his Holly answered the phone? He must remember to tell her not to pick up the line. But then, David had said it would all be over soon, so what was he worried about?

Charles sighed mightily, punched his pillow a good three times, then settled down. With closed eyes, he focused on work. On Riverside. Only Riverside didn't stay Riverside. He turned into a voluptuous creature who hadn't a stitch on.

Madness. How was Charles supposed to sleep when his mind was in the gutter?

He turned over, punched his pillow again and flung his arm over his other pillow. Only it wasn't a pillow, it was Jane.

Holly.

Jane.

What difference did it make? She was in his bed. Right now. Right next to him. Wearing...?

He moaned. And felt her hand on his arm.

SHE'D BEEN SECONDS from sleep. Smack dab in between awareness and unconsciousness, when the world hardly seems real at all.

But Charley hitting her in the head had reversed the process. The way he moaned, she'd have thought he'd hit his own head. "Charley, what's wrong?"

"What are you doing here?"

"I was about to fall asleep."

"But you're not supposed to be here."

"Where should I be?"

"In the guest room."

"You have a guest room?"

"Yes. And it's all made up for you."

"Why?" She felt him pull away. Shift. Finally, she opened one eye and saw he'd sat up.

"Why? Because we're not— You're not— It's not right."

"When did you get so old-fashioned?"

"That's not the issue. The issue is that we agreed we would wait, and now look at yourself. You're here."

"Relax, Charley. It's not as if I was going to rape you or anything. In fact, if you hadn't been such a big lug, we would both be sound asleep by now." She closed her eyes again. "Lie down. Relax. I don't bite."

"You don't bite. Ha. That's very amusing. You don't bite. Biting has nothing to do with it."

Sighing once more, this time with resignation, she sat up, too. "Has nothing to do with what?"

"You. Me. This."

"Do you *ever* stop thinking about sex?"

"No! I mean, yes. Of course. I always stop thinking about sex."

She reached behind her to the lamp on the night table and turned it on, wincing in the sudden brightness, then focusing on Charley. "You want to try that one again, sailor?"

He didn't seem to be too happy about the light. In fact, he'd pulled the comforter up to his chin. She was reminded of virginal girls in old western movies. Giggling didn't help things, but once that image was in her mind there was no stopping.

"It's not funny Ja—Holly."

"Funny jolly? What does that mean?"

"Nothing. Turn off the light. Then go to your room."

"Won't that make it hard to see?"

His eyelids lowered halfway. Not in a sexy way. Rather, in a way that stated quite clearly that if she didn't stop her cute little remarks, he was going to strangle her with the belt to his robe.

"Sorry."

"I think it would be best if you went to the back bedroom."

"Fine. Sleep alone. I don't care. I'm too tired to care." She threw the covers back and prepared to stomp out dramatically, slamming the door behind her. His gasp stopped her cold. "What?"

"You're not wearing pajamas."

She looked down. He was right. She wasn't wearing pajamas. She didn't like pajamas. They were okay to wear to bed, just not to sleep. She'd worn her usual attire—panties and a tank top. No muss, no fuss. "Charley, stop staring like that. It's not like I'm naked."

"You might as well be."

She shook her head, fully, utterly awake now. "How long has it been since you've had sex? With a woman, I mean?"

He cleared his throat. Then did it again. "It's late. I'm sure you're tired. The guest room is all made up for you."

She gave him one last pout before she shrugged her legs over the side of the bed. "Right. Like I'm going to sleep now. I hope there's a TV in the guest room. With cable."

"I don't have a television in that room."

"Where do you have a television?"

"In here."

"That's it?"

"I don't need another television elsewhere."

She stood, turned to face him. "So what am I supposed to do? My head hurts too much to read, and I don't knit."

"If you lie down and close your eyes, you'll be asleep before you know it."

"That actually works for you?"

"Sometimes."

She crooked her right brow.

"Well, it works in theory."

Her gaze went to his chest and the blanket, still up to his chin. "Charley, it's okay. You don't have to keep hiding your goodies from me. Your virtue is safe."

"My goodies?"

"You must have something good under there to be hiding it so fiercely."

He dropped the comforter. His pajamas were cotton, with blue and white stripes. A little monogram adorned each cuff. They looked as if they'd been purchased from the Sears Catalog circa 1800.

"What?"

"Nothing."

"That look is not nothing."

"Those are some hot pj's you got there, Charley."

"There's nothing wrong with them."

"Nope. Not a thing."

"They're sensible."

"Absolutely."

"And comfortable."

"No doubt."

"So why are you looking at me that way?"

She leaned forward, placing her palms flat on the bed. Gravity did its thing and made the front of her tank top hang open. He was getting one heck of a gander at *her* goodies. "I'm looking at you because of those pajamas," she said, moving one hand forward, then lifting one knee onto the bed. "I was fine before, but now, I don't think I can stop myself."

The other knee came up. She was now on all fours, top sagging in the breeze. Her breasts, which hardly ever moved much, swung from side to side as she inched her way closer to Charley's side of the bed.

He couldn't keep his eyes off her. Well, at least a certain part of her. Men and boobs. Go figure. Hers were of the medium persuasion, C cups on a good day. But the way he was staring, you'd think she was Jayne Mansfield.

"Stop that."

"I can't. Don't you understand? The pajamas— they're bigger than you and me. I'm helpless. I must have you."

"Cut it out, Holly."

She took another swaying step with her right hand and leg. "The stripes. They're..." She growled like a tiger, finding it incredibly hard not to laugh.

Charley looked as if someone had spiked the fruit punch. His mouth hung open, the comforter was now back under his chin and his eyes had widened. But if he'd been truly appalled, wouldn't he have averted his gaze?

"Charley?"

"What?"

"Are you absolutely, positively certain you want to wait?"

"For what?"

"The wedding night, silly."

"Holly. I'm warning you."

"You are, huh?"

"This is not amusing."

"The heck you say."

He scooted over. She kept on going. Baby steps, but they'd get her there. He scooted some more. She moved another inch. She had him now. He couldn't scoot over any more. There wasn't any bed left.

"You stop right there or I'll...I'll—"

She didn't stop. She moved that one final inch. For a moment she thought he was going to lunge at her, grab her as he'd done in the closet. But he didn't. He scooted. Right off the bed.

She tried to grab him on his way down, but she missed. He made a really loud thump.

She hurried the rest of the way over and found him sitting up, staring straight ahead. "Charley?"

He didn't answer.

"Are you all right?"

"Yes." His reply could have frosted all the glass in the apartment with its chill.

"I tried to warn you."

"That's quite all right. You don't need to concern yourself with me."

"I don't?"

He finally looked up at her. "Would you be so kind as to pass me my pillow?"

She did, never taking her eyes off him. When he took it, he nodded a polite, gentrified thanks. Then he put the pillow on the floor, yanked the comforter up, lay down and closed his eyes.

"Charley?"

"Yes?"

"Isn't that a little uncomfortable?"

"No."

She sighed. "I don't know who's crazier here. Me, for dropping everything to be with you again, or you for not wanting to do anything about it."

His eyes opened. "If I say I'm the crazy one, will you shut the light and go to sleep?"

"Fine. Have it your own way. I'm going to the other room. I just don't understand you, Charley. It's like you're not yourself."

She jumped off the bed and walked to the door. She even got to slam it, just the way she'd planned. But the moment she was outside in the hall, she wanted back in. It was lonely without him. Lonely, and a little scary.

9

HE'D SLEPT THROUGH breakfast. Through Ben's knock on the door. He hadn't been first in the office and he'd slept through Frank Toyamichi's call.

It was nine-fifteen, the latest Charles had ever slept. Even when he'd been on vacation. The reason was clear: he hadn't fallen asleep until about six. But that was an excuse, nothing more.

Ellen must already be here. Had she found Holly?

Holly. Not anymore. She'd probably be Jane this morning, and that presented another set of problems.

Hoisting himself out of bed, he headed for his bathroom. As he showered, the problems hit him as hard and fast as the water. Was she awake? If she was awake, would she remember yesterday? She'd be humiliated by her behavior. He'd have to dismiss it as nothing. But what about his kiss? How was he going to explain that? David. He'd call David, ask him to come over. David would help her understand.

Damn, if she was awake, she might not even know where she was. What if she was scared to death? Cowering in some corner? Or what if she'd called the police?

Charles washed in record time, barely rinsed, then got out of the shower and into his towel. Shaving would have to wait.

If she wasn't Jane, then what? He couldn't have her here another day. He had to go to the office. Surely she shouldn't be left alone.

Ellen could watch her. Ellen was a sensible woman; she'd understand, and she'd take care of her. At least, he hoped so.

Finished in the bath, he went to his closet and was jolted again at what she'd bought, and how she'd shoved all of his things aside. What about all this stuff? It could be returned. But then maybe that wasn't the right thing to do. Maybe he should let her keep her new things. They couldn't have cost that much.

He dressed hurriedly, cringing at the wrinkles in his shirt, then headed out to assess the situation. Oddly enough, he found himself hoping she hadn't remembered. Which was crazy. She was nothing but trouble. She'd turned everything upside down. All he wanted was his life back. His nice, orderly life.

She wasn't in the hallway. He headed for the guest room, treading as lightly as possible. The last thing he wanted to do was scare her. A few more steps and he was at the door. The open door. He leaned forward, craning his neck so he could see inside.

No Jane. Holly. Neither one. And the bed was made. Okay. He headed back down the hall, this time faster, and into the living room. Even before he could see into the kitchen, he heard them. Two feminine voices, one older, gruffer, one young and eager. Who was he going to find chatting with Ellen?

His pace slowed as he passed the couch. Ellen stood by the sink, a cup of coffee in her hand. She wore a broad grin, one he'd never seen before. But he couldn't see *her*.

He hesitated. Maybe the smart thing to do was just leave. Get out of here. Call David to come and clean up this mess.

Or was he just being a coward?

If Charles turned to the left, he could be out the door and in the elevator before anyone had a chance to see him. It would be cowardly. No doubt about that. But he could learn to live with the shame.

If he turned to the right... A wave of trepidation washed through him, shaking him as he stood. His heart had gone into fourth, his jacket was suddenly too warm, not to mention his clammy hands. It wasn't a girly kind of fear or anything. Maybe excitement was a better word. Oh, no. No, no. That would be ludicrous. The woman was nothing but trouble. He'd tried to be a Good Samaritan, that's all. The kissing? Not his fault. He'd been taken by surprise.

But if someone pointed a gun at his head and forced him to tell the truth about his current state, excitement would have to be included. So would trepidation, so it wasn't as if he was completely nuts.

"Charley, are you going to stand there all day or are you going to kiss me good-morning?"

He jerked his head up so fast he almost got whiplash. He had his answer, all right. She was Holly. And she turned him on like a Waring blender.

"Well?"

At least she wasn't in the panties and tank top from last night. This morning found her in her jeans again, but instead of the bare-midriff sweater she'd worn last night, she'd chosen a large white sweater that covered too much. The only good part about it was that when she moved, his gaze went right to the parts of her that stuck out. For all it hid, the sweater had some sly moves.

She sighed and walked over to him. "First you sleep in, then you stare at me like I'm an apparition. You're not catching a cold, are you?"

He shook his head.

"Good. Then it's all right for me to do this." Her hands went to either side of his face, holding him steady as she leaned in for a kiss that started off modestly but built to a crescendo in three seconds flat.

His body reacted, of course. It had no choice. As she kissed, she rubbed against him. Back and forth, right where it counted. He wanted to push her away, stop this blatant display, but when his hands gripped her shoulders, he pulled her closer, instead. Damn it, why couldn't she have been Jane?

She purred as her hands slipped down to his neck and then down some more, and he cursed his suit jacket for diluting the effect of those hands on his shoulders. His grip on her arms tightened, and if it wasn't for the tiny voice of sanity somewhere in the recesses of his mind, he'd have hurt her badly. He let her go, but she didn't release him. She wasn't done yet.

"Well, I'll be painted pink and stuck with feathers."

Charles pushed Holly away, more forcefully than he should have, at the sound of Ellen's mystified voice. The heat of embarrassment boiled to his face.

Holly looked from him to Ellen. She shrugged, shook her head and smiled as if the two of them were sharing a familiar scenario, one in which he starred as the fall guy—the ridiculous man among women who know more, who feel more, who intuit more. If he were the type, he would have given them a piece of his mind in no uncertain terms. But he wasn't prone to crassness.

"Excuse me, Holly," he said, remembering the correct appellation at the last moment. "But I'm late for work."

"Don't be testy, Charley. You look adorable when you blush."

He raised a warning brow.

"At least come in and have breakfast. Ellen made a scrumptious frittata."

Frittata? What was the matter with her? She knew what he liked for breakfast.

Ellen must have realized she was in the soup because suddenly a cup needed washing as he walked into the kitchen. The table was set, yet his newspaper was missing from its proper place.

Holly scurried past him, and a few seconds later, the *Times* was in front of his place setting. "Better?" she asked.

"Better."

"Good. But can you do me a favor?"

He was afraid to answer. "What kind of a favor?"

"A little teeny one." To illustrate, she held two fingers a hairsbreadth apart.

"Go on."

"Can you read the paper later? We need to talk."

Behind him, Ellen coughed. It wasn't a real cough. It was a cough meant to disguise laughter.

"What do we need to talk about?"

"The wedding, silly. You think it's just going to happen by magic? We need to make plans."

Charles opened his mouth, then realized he had no idea what to say. He wasn't going to marry her, so he was loath to help her make wedding plans. On the other hand, she was still deeply affected by the blow on her head, which meant she probably knew that she had to arrange the ceremony immediately.

David.

"Will you excuse me for a moment?" Charles said, dazzling her with his best smile.

She hesitated. "Okay."

"I just have to make a quick call. Perhaps you can get a plate ready for me? And coffee?"

Her face lit up, and again he was struck by the contrasts—the innate wisdom in her eyes, the voluptuous mouth, the girlish curls and baby-smooth cheeks.

David.

Charles held up a finger, then turned on his heel. Before she could say another word, he was out of the kitchen and halfway to his bedroom. He needed privacy for this call. Not just because he didn't want Holly to hear something she shouldn't, but because he intended to curse his best buddy to hell and back.

"Isn't he wonderful?" Holly went to the cupboard and pulled down a plate.

"Yes, I think he is rather wonderful," Ellen said.

She'd been there since six-thirty, and she'd tried to convince Holly to wake Charley, but Holly had stood firm. The man needed his sleep. Yesterday had been a momentous day for both of them, and momentous days were extremely draining.

Ellen had given in, but only because she wanted to ask a hundred questions.

"I can't get over it," the older woman said. "The way he described you, I never would have guessed."

"How?"

"He said you were sensible. A good hostess. He didn't mention that smile of yours. Or the mischief in your eyes."

"When?"

"When what?"

"Did he describe me?"

Ellen flushed a bit and got busy slicing the frittata. "He didn't exactly describe you to me."

"Pardon?"

"I overheard him on the phone. When I was cleaning."

"Ah, I see. Did you happen to hear who was on the other end?"

She shook her head. "Nope. But my guess would be Dr. David." Ellen handed the plate to Holly, then went to the coffeepot and poured two cups, one for herself and one for Charley.

"You come here every day?"

"Five days a week."

"To clean?"

"I do that. But I also do the cooking. I go shopping for him. I pick up his dry cleaning, things like that."

"Things a wife would do."

"I suppose so." Ellen took a long sip of the hot coffee. "I suppose, too, that I ought to be looking for another job."

"Why?"

"When you get married, you won't need me anymore."

"Please. You're a part of the family. Of course we'll need you. Especially when the babies come."

A masculine cough made her spin around.

"Babies?" Charley had that pasty look again. "What babies?"

"Come sit. Eat before it all gets cold."

"I'm not hungry."

"You will be once you taste this." She sat down next to him and got comfy, pulling one foot up on the chair, her knee under her chin.

Charley gave her the brow, which she was beginning to dislike. But he sat, and he lifted his fork. She didn't say boo until he finally took a mouthful of the egg, cheese, bacon and mushroom concoction. He chewed tentatively at first, but then his infamous brows rose in an expression of surprise and delight.

"I told you so."

"But you haven't told me what babies you were talking about."

"Ours."

"We don't have any."

"But we will. I want at least four. Two girls and two boys."

He choked on a piece of egg, and Ellen gave him a whack on the back that took him so by surprise his fork flew halfway across the room.

"Wow," Holly said, clapping. "What do you do for an encore?"

"I go to work." He pushed back from the table even though he'd hardly eaten, and he hadn't touched his coffee. "Now."

"But—"

"Now. I'm terribly late as it is." He got up, his expression serious as a funeral. "I want you to stay in. Do you understand? No running around. At all. Ellen will be here with you, and after she leaves, it'll only be a half hour till I get home."

"And how do you expect me to plan a wedding if I'm stuck in the house?"

"That's what phones are for."

"Do you have a computer?"

He didn't answer. In fact, the way his eyes skittered around, looking at everything in the room but her, she'd swear that he was trying to avoid the question. But then she remembered. "Oh, yeah. It's in the bedroom. There are tons and tons of wedding sites." She nodded to herself. "I can handle that." Once again, she focused on him. "But I don't understand why you're making such a fuss. I'm a grown woman. I go out by myself all the time."

Once more, his eyes did that crazy avoidance dance, and this time, for an added bonus, he cleared his throat and ran his hand through his hair.

"Love," Ellen said from by the sink, "with that lump on your head, you'd better take it easy today. It looks nasty."

Holly's fingers went to the bruise, and she winced as

she explored it. "I can't believe I don't remember how I got this. Isn't that too weird?"

"It's perfectly natural," Ellen said. "So don't worry about it. Just stay here and plan away."

Holly nodded, more to avoid the brow than anything else. But her reward was swift and sweet. He smiled.

What a smile he had. It changed him utterly. He was good-looking no matter how you sliced it, but when he smiled, she could see the boy in him. The charming rascal instead of the brooding businessman. This was her Charley; the other was fine for the rest of the world. She was a complete sucker for that smile.

It was short-lived, however. Charles straightened his stodgy tie. She really ought to do him a favor and get him some ties with life in them. The Net. *Mais oui.* She still had his credit card. Somehow she knew he had an enormous credit limit.

"Okay." She stood and gave him a quick kiss on the lips. Then another. Only this one wasn't so hasty. This one took, and Charley kissed her back. His hand went to her neck to make sure she stayed put, and then he let her know what was what. His tongue, that talented little devil, teased and swirled like a magician's wand. By the time he let her go, the world had started to spin.

"Ellen," he said, turning to his housekeeper as if he hadn't just curled Holly's toes. "I appreciate you looking after Holly."

"It's my pleasure."

"And I'm wondering if you could come with me for a moment. I want to show you a stain on one of my shirts."

Ellen nodded, and they left the room. Charley didn't even say goodbye. How could he kiss her like that and then be so blasé? Holly wondered. It didn't make sense.

She sat down and pulled his plate over in front of her, then picked up her knife. She'd already had a piece of the frittata, but she wanted more. She cut a perfect little square from the middle of his slice and carefully brought it to her plate. Then she cut the square into littler squares. When she was satisfied, she retrieved his fork and ate the pieces one by one, chewing slowly, luxuriating in the intimacy of sharing a fork.

Life didn't get much better than this. It was perfect. Exactly how she'd dreamed it would be. Had there ever been a girl as lucky as her?

CHARLES CHECKED THE DOOR again, certain Holly was going to barge in any second. He'd tried to explain the situation to Ellen, but she looked more confused now than when he'd begun.

"So, you're not getting married?"

"No. We're not."

"But you want me to help her plan the wedding."

"Yes."

Ellen nodded, but he knew her well enough to translate the pacifying gesture. What she was really saying was that he was a fool, but she was too polite to tell him to his face.

"Look, David's going to be here in an hour or so. He's going to talk with her. Figure out why this delusion hasn't ended. You can ask him any questions you want."

"I'll do that."

"Thank you." Charles patted her shoulder, and the look she gave him this time let him know that was wrong, too. The best thing he could do was get the hell out of here. Go to his office. Running a hundred-million-dollar business was a hell of a lot easier than dealing with women.

10

HOLLY CLICKED to the Martha Stewart wedding Web site and spent a long dreamy moment imagining herself in a Vera Wang wedding gown. The dress was so much like her fantasies it was scary. White, of course, with an A-line skirt, empire waist, pearls covering the bodice. The sleek lines and the décolletage were just sexy enough. And the veil! It was more a tiara than anything else, and it would look great with her curls.

Sighing, she tore her gaze away to read the articles, but bookmarked the page for later, as well. Of course, Martha had nothing but elegant advice. It took Holly close to forty minutes to read everything, and as she did, she took notes. Flowers, the wedding party, the minister, the reception. So much to do in such a short amount of time!

Unfortunately, there wasn't an available room at the Algonquin, her first choice. Nor at the Four Seasons. But the Westminster Regent, one of the finest hotels in Manhattan, came through. Only after she'd mentioned Charley's name, though. They'd had a cancellation, and she booked the sucker right there on the phone. She'd been right about Charley's credit card limit—she made the deposit with absolutely no fuss.

They had an appointment on Saturday with the banquet manager to go over the plans, so she was determined to work out every detail before then.

After a click to Yahoo! Holly found another wedding Web site, this one with a checklist and a timeline. She adjusted the pillow behind her back as she read. Charley's bed was an ideal spot to do her research. He had everything to make working on the laptop easy—a bed tray that fit over her legs and held the computer steady, a great light source, a place to put her coffee cup and even room for her notebook. But mostly she liked working here because it was Charley's bed.

His scent was on his pillow, in the sheets, and every time she became aware of it she took in a deep, deep breath. She wanted him inside her, and if she had to settle for this, so be it. Of course she respected his wish to wait for the wedding night, but it wouldn't hurt her feelings any if he changed his mind. In fact, she was going to do her best to help sway him in the other direction.

Enough about that, though. She went back to reading the Web site. Five minutes later, the doorbell rang. Was it Charley? Her heart pumped wildly with the notion until she realized he had a key to his own apartment. But her curiosity was piqued, so she set the bed tray aside and headed for the living room. Ellen nodded when she saw her, then headed for the kitchen. Holly's attention went to their guest. "David!"

His warm smile made him especially handsome. She held out her hands as he approached, and he took them. Then she kissed his cheeks, European style. He was the one to hug her, but she returned the embrace with fervor.

"I hope I'm not intruding."

"You? David, you're welcome here anytime."

He grinned. "I know. I was just being polite."

"Well, stop it. There will be no politeness in this house."

"Charley is a lucky man."

Her cheeks heated in a blush, knowing the compliment was heartfelt.

"You have a few minutes to spare? Maybe a cup of coffee for a wandering shrink?"

"Of course." She took his hand again and led him to the dining room. He sat in Charley's chair. "How do you like your coffee?"

"I've got it," Ellen called from the kitchen. "You just sit yourself down."

Holly did, in her usual fashion, knee under chin. A moment later, Ellen came out bearing two mugs. Holly took advantage and gave David a long perusal. How come such a good-looking guy, a doctor no less, wasn't married? He hadn't ever been, she knew, although he'd had a couple of serious relationships. There was something about him that made her want to take care of him, even though he was considered one of the most promising young psychiatrists in the country.

Maybe it was his hair. Brown, slightly wavy, it was too long on the collar, and it looked as if he'd used his fingers instead of a comb this morning. No, actually, that made him look sexy.

His eyes? Definitely not a problem. They shone with intelligence and compassion. It wasn't his face, which was youthful, yet serious. Or his clothes, tailored and elegant. So it must be something from his insides.

Something that belied his polished exterior. He needed someone. She'd have to work on that.

Ellen left again but returned a moment later with a carafe and a small pitcher of cream. "I'm going to leave for a little while," she said. "I have some shopping to do." She turned to Holly. "Did you think of anything else?"

"If you have time, some crackers and cheese would be lovely. But the decorations come first, all right?"

Ellen nodded. "I'll be back quick as a wink."

Holly waved a goodbye, a part of her wishing she was going, too, then turned her whole attention to David.

CHARLES STOOD BEHIND his chair, staring out at the city beneath him. He loved Manhattan. Especially in winter. To him, the crowds were the lifeblood of the city, coursing through veins of winding streets. Healthy, active, alive. He liked to walk, although he had precious little time to do that anymore. He'd traveled a great deal in his life, but no where else called him like this city. Not that he minded having his place in the Hamptons. Everyone needed to get away sometimes. But this was home.

It was already noon, and he'd gotten nothing accomplished. Nothing. With the singular exception of letting his human resources manager know he needed a good secretary until Mrs. Robinson came back. The woman who had her desk today wasn't half-bad. She'd given him coffee immediately, reported his phone calls, then canceled his appointments for the rest of the afternoon.

A comment she'd made when he arrived kept pop-

ping into his mind. It wasn't an unusual remark, just
that they'd all been worried when he didn't come in at
his usual time. He'd apologized, and she'd gone away
happy, but then it had occurred to him that someone
was undoubtedly worried about Jane. David hadn't
had much luck reaching her family.

Charles had already checked for her messages here.
No one had called except the blood bank, wanting to
know when she was going to make her regular dona-
tion. He'd looked in her desk for a personal phone
book, a Rolodex. He'd found nothing but a mass of cut-
up Christmas cards, several miniature candy bars,
work files and a spare set of keys. He felt sure one of
those keys was to her apartment, and that had kept his
mind occupied most of the morning.

It wasn't right to snoop. He wouldn't like it if someone went through his belongings when he wasn't
there. But this was a medical emergency, wasn't it?
What if there were frantic messages on her answering
machine at home and he could get in touch with her
loved ones to assure them that she was fine?

David had said she had three sisters. They must be
wondering where she'd been last night. And what if
she had pets? They'd need to be fed, and if she had a
dog...

That decided it for him. He turned and pressed the
intercom button.

"Yes, Mr. Warren?"

"I'm going out for a few hours. In fact, I'm not sure
I'll be back today."

"Yes, sir. Is there anything I should do while you're
gone?"

"Just answer the phones. Thank you." He released the button, got his coat and her keys, and headed for Harlem.

DAVID LISTENED with half an ear as Jane went on about the wedding. The way her eyes lit up was far more interesting to him. The animation in her face, the innocent joy of her expression...she was a lovely girl. She had been as long as he'd known her. But as Jane, she'd walked with slightly stooped shoulders, as if afraid to be too big, too noticeable. She'd talked softly, barely met his gaze.

Holly was a whole different story. She was all the things Jane could be, if only she had the confidence. What worried him was that Holly was a temporary visitor. Would this experience help Jane blossom? Would she even remember it?

"So I think traditional colors are what Charley would want," she was saying.

"What do you want?"

She grinned. "I want sea-foam green and the palest salmon."

"Really."

"It's gorgeous, I swear. Even though it sounds fussy, it's so perfect it would make you cry."

"Then you should have sea-foam green and palest salmon."

"I don't know..."

"Do you mind if I change the subject?"

She shook her head, setting her curls in motion.

"How are you feeling?"

"Me? Fine. Why?"

He nodded toward her head.

"Oh, that. It only hurts if I press on it. It's peculiar, though, that I can't remember where I got it. You'd think I'd remember something like that."

"Not necessarily. Often with blunt trauma, there's a bit of amnesia."

"Amnesia. Cool."

He shook his head. "You're a real piece of work, you know that? But an extraordinary piece of work."

"Moi?" She waved away the compliment.

"Can I ask you something?"

"Anything."

"Why do you think Charles put the ad in the magazine?"

She blinked rapidly, her expressive face suddenly passive. David was embarking on a risky journey, he knew, and it made him nervous. The last thing in the world he wanted was for Jane to get hurt. But he needed to know the situation with her amnesia, and if she needed more help than he could give her.

"He...he didn't know how to find me. I was away."

"Away?"

She nodded, but she didn't look at him. Her coffee mug had become fascinating.

"That's right," David said. "You were in Europe."

"Yes. Of course. I was in Europe, so he couldn't have called me, could he? I mean, I didn't leave any phone number."

"Right. Actually, though, I was wondering more about why he put the ad in the magazine now. Why not a year ago? Two years ago?"

"He wasn't ready."

Her voice had changed. The singsong, vibrant cadence of Holly was gone; in its place was the subdued, almost timid voice of Jane.

"Ready?"

She nodded. "He wasn't ready to settle down. But as soon as he was, he knew it was going to be us."

"What about you?"

"I've always known it was going to be us. From the first moment I saw him."

"So you weren't worried when you were away."

"Oh, no. Not at all. It's Charley, remember? My Charley."

"What is it about him?"

"What do you mean?"

"What is it that makes him your Charley? That kept you in love all this time?"

Her shoulders relaxed, and she even put her leg down so she was sitting normally, not all hunched up in the tiniest possible space. If he was correct, David thought, this would be the easiest question for her to answer. Her love for Charles—Charley—was as much a part of Jane as it was of Holly.

"You know. You're his best friend."

"But I'm not a woman. I'm not you."

She nodded. Sipped her coffee. Smiled in a mysterious way. "He's very brave, and yet he doesn't know it."

"Brave?"

"He took over his business with such single-mindedness. Nothing was going to stop him. I'm not sure, but I think he wanted to prove to his father that he could do it."

"Do you know much about his father?"

Her right shoulder rose in a half shrug. "He doesn't talk about him much. I know he died too young. And that he was with..."

"Ah, so you know about that."

"Not really. Rumors mostly."

"It was hard on Charley. His father was his role model. He was incredibly proud of his dad. He couldn't really face the fact that his father was human."

"I understand."

David hesitated. Normally he would never consider divulging the circumstances surrounding George Warren's death. But something told him it was important for Jane to know. It wasn't often these feelings came along, but he'd learned to listen to them when they did. He'd never tell anyone, but it was these intermittent flashes of insight that made him a good psychiatrist. And he'd never had more flashes than when he was around Jane.

"Charley's father died in a hotel room. He wasn't alone. And he wasn't with Charley's mother."

"Oh. Oh, dear."

"It caused something of a sensation, although it only made the *Post*, not the *Times*. Charley couldn't believe it. It crushed him."

"Who was she?"

"She was a nice young lady. A painter. She was very beautiful, very artistic, and she didn't know one thing about business."

"I can see where a man like him might need a...break. But what about his mother? I mean, Charley's mother?"

"She was the picture of grace under pressure. She'd known about Tina for a long while. She didn't like it, but she had her reasons for putting up with it. But her husband's death hit her very hard. He was such a young man, and seemingly in the best of health."

"That's so sad."

David nodded. He poured himself another cup of coffee, although what he really wanted was something to eat. He wasn't willing to stop the process, though. "It got worse. It seems that the company wasn't half as strong as everyone thought. There were some serious discrepancies in the books, and Charley had to do some fancy footwork to get the IRS to let him work things out. I'll give the guy credit. He made a plan, and he stuck to it. Paid off his father's debts in two years, and kept right on going. Now the company is worth more than ever."

"That's good about paying off the debts, but I don't think it's so great that he kept on like that."

"Why not?"

"Because Charley's forgotten how to have fun. He doesn't know there's another kind of satisfaction. That there's laughter and passion and friendships and adventure."

"And that's where you come in?"

She gave David a little grin. "Yep."

"Do you know what?"

"What?"

"I concur."

"Do you?"

He nodded. "You're what my mother would call a mensch."

"What's that?"

"It's a good person. Someone who does wonderful things without expecting anything in return."

"I expect things from Charley."

"What?"

"His love. And his commitment."

"Is there more?"

"About what I expect?"

"No, about why you love him."

"There's a million little things. How he loves to read. That he's so damn compulsive about his closet. That he sends people to watch after his mother."

"He's not all sweetness and light, you know."

"Yes. I do. He's human, all right. His temper." She rolled her eyes. "That's not pretty. And he gets so rigid sometimes. He's so focused he doesn't notice the people around him much."

"He doesn't?"

"It's okay. He doesn't ignore them intentionally. He doesn't mean to hurt them."

"But they do get hurt."

She changed again. It was a fascinating phenomenon, one he'd like to study further. She wasn't a multiple personality, but she had some of the characteristics—the body posture, the mannerisms. What he understood was that both the timid and the brave were in Jane. She didn't have to be Holly to be outspoken, to be so confident. But it would take some doing to convince Jane of that.

When she came out of this, he hoped she'd remember how strong she'd felt. How sure of herself. He could help her see that she needn't go into hiding again.

In his considered opinion, she was all right. She had some tough things to go through in the next few days, but she'd make it. And if everything went as planned, she'd have Charley there to help with every step. And Charley? He'd never know that with every kindness he extended to Jane, he was healing, too.

They were both wounded. And they could heal each other. David saw it so clearly, it made him a little sad for himself. That's what he wanted. A woman as good for him as Jane was for Charley.

Someday. Sure. Someday he'd have it all.

"David?"

"Yes?"

"Are you as hungry as I am?"

"More."

She sprang from the chair, and he followed, knowing whatever they were going to have for lunch would be unusual, eclectic, wonderful. Damn, but Charley was a lucky man.

11

CHARLES UNLOCKED THE DOOR on the sixth floor of the old building. He'd knocked, just in case someone was there, but the only answer he'd gotten was a suspicious glance from the woman across the way. When he'd tried to talk to her, she'd slammed her door in his face.

He entered Jane's apartment. It wasn't what he expected. In fact, it was barely an apartment. Everything was squished together in an impossibly tight space, the worst of it the bathtub in the kitchen. He'd never seen anything like it. Never imagined Jane in a place like this.

All his life, he'd lived in luxury. In fact, he could have afforded a bigger penthouse, or a whole building, for that matter. But his place suited him. It was big enough for him to spread out, and small enough that it wasn't a distraction.

He slowly toured the miniscule living room-kitchen-dining room-bathing area, which took him about two minutes, then he found the bathroom, which was no more than a water closet, and the bedroom, which had only enough room for a twin bed and a dresser. There was no sign of a pet, not even a fish. But in the larger room there was a Christmas tree. A balding, aged, crooked tree, hardly deserving of the appellation, but as he got closer he realized Jane had decorated the ugly thing with a great deal of loving attention. Handmade bows, little cloth pockets holding candy canes, a popcorn string and several pictures dangled from the scraggly branches. He recognized two people in the photos: Darra, her model sister, and surprisingly, himself.

It was an old photo from the *New York Times*, taken when he'd gone to one of those omnipresent fundraisers. Jane had cut it out of the paper and had it laminated. She couldn't possibly have done that after her accident.

He let go of the hanging photo and the whole tree bobbled. But his attention was already elsewhere. The walls. One had at least a dozen pegs, each bearing a hat of some kind—knit, straw, berets, cowboy, all hung up in an artful display. Clever. Very clever.

The opposite wall was just as unique. The center of the wall had been framed with black paint, and within the large square was an intricate collage. Intrigued, he moved closer and starting from the upper right corner, he studied the pictures. He recognized her family, at least who he assumed was her family from the Christmas tree photos. There were several cutouts of a dog, a rather mangy looking Lab. The Chrysler Building took up some considerable space, as did pictures of Central Park.

And then there were pictures of him again. From magazines, from newspapers. She'd cut out every public photo he'd ever been in. Some of them years old. Where had she gotten them? *Why* had she gotten them?

A crush? Until yesterday, he'd barely spoken to her. Hardly noticed her. She'd never indicated in any way that she was interested in him. Or maybe she had, and he hadn't picked up on it?

It was terribly confusing. But he couldn't stand here all day. He needed to find her address book, make his calls, then ring David.

He headed for the bedroom and opened the dresser drawers one at a time. Nothing in there but clothes. After he pushed in the bottom drawer, he went back to the top. Feeling guilty as hell, he opened that one again. He just had to make sure he hadn't missed anything, that a phone book wasn't hidden underneath her colorful panties, so small he could hardly believe they were for a grown person. Unfortunately, after last night, he could picture her far too clearly wearing each scrap of material.

He shoved the drawer home, appalled at his indiscretion. At his motives.

He'd come here for more than an address book. He wanted to understand who Jane was. Why she'd turned to him in her troubled state. She wasn't his type, not at all the kind of woman he'd have given a second look, but the way he felt when she was near...

It was crazy. The whole business. What in hell was he doing searching underwear drawers in Harlem? Turning on his heel, he went to her bed and noticed the edge of a book peeking out from under the sheets. He threw the covers back, but instead of an address book, he found a journal.

He had no business looking at it. And he wouldn't. He covered it with the blanket, then did a systematic and thorough search of the rest of the apartment. No phone book. No laptop. No Rolodex, no Day-Timer. Not even one message on her answering machine.

He didn't like it, but he went back to the bedroom and pulled out her journal. There had to be phone numbers in it, unless she kept all that information in her head. Or perhaps her purse, which was God knows where.

He sat down, sinking quite low into the mattress, and pulled off his gloves. He looked at the last few pages, but they were blank. Then he turned to the front of the book, and he hit pay dirt. There was a list of numbers on the flyleaf: Mother, Felicity, Darra, Pru, Aunt Sylvia, Granny, Office. He would call her mother first, of course.

The phone was in the other room. With considerable difficulty, given the condition of the bed, he rose, then took the book with him to make his calls. It was freezing in the apartment, and he wished he could put his gloves back on, but he'd have to wait. He sat on a straight-backed chair, got the phone and hit the first three numbers. Then he hung up. What was he supposed to say?

Should he tell them about her amnesia? Yes, he'd better. It wasn't fair for them not to know. Especially her mother.

He dialed that number until he got a ring.

A woman with a Spanish accent answered.

"May I speak with Mrs. Dobson?"

"Mrs. Dobson is no here."

"When will she be back?"

"Not for a long time. She in Europe with the Mr. and her daughter."

"Thank you." Charles hung up, guessing that the daughter in question was Prudence. Somewhere in the back of his mind he seemed to remember she was on tour. He called the number for Felicity, but she wasn't there, either. She was in California. Next was Darra. The woman on the billboard.

"Hello?" Her voice sounded raspy, sleepy, as if he'd awakened her.

"Is this Darra Dobson?"

"Yeah. Who are you?"

"My name is Charles Warren."

"Wait a sec."

He heard a loud clunk. She must have dropped the phone. Then he heard a match struck, a sharp inhale, a cough. "You still there?"

"Yes," he said. "I am."

"Did Jane give you this number?"

"In a way. She's the reason I'm calling."

"She told you about the restaurant opening, right? You can make it?"

"What restaurant?"

There was another sharp inhale. "My restaurant, Haute Couture."

"No, she didn't. You see—"

"She said you were going to be out of the country."

"When?"

"This week."

"Be that as it may, the reason I'm calling is because Jane's had an acci—"

"Damn, I've got someone on the other line. Can you hold?"

"Yes."

She clicked off and he was left with dead air. The question, of course, was should he hang around until she got back on the line? She didn't seem terribly interested in Jane. In fact, he doubted she could be less interested. But she was Jane's sister. Having no siblings himself, he wasn't absolutely sure Darra's reaction wasn't normal. Although his gut told him no.

He headed back to Jane's bedroom, still listening to nothing but a low hum. Once there, he took his time looking around the room. There were pictures on the wall in here, too, mostly cut from magazines. Different shots, some of people, some of buildings, mostly objects, like a photo of a tombstone, an elephant, clouds in a blue sky. It was a hodgepodge, and he wondered if she was preparing another collage. He went to the bed and touched her top sheet. The satiny luxury of fine Egyptian cotton was instantly recognizable. The fitted sheet had an entirely different feel, and when he pushed the covers back he saw a large picture of Wonder Woman in full regalia.

He moved the phone to his other ear and looked at his watch. Darra had been on the other line for at least three minutes. He'd give her fifteen more seconds.

At seventeen seconds, he hung up. He'd done what he could. But Jane was clearly in better hands with him than she would be with her sister. Poor kid.

He went back to the dining room-cum-bath and looked at the journal. While he'd been in the other room, a few pages had turned, the one on the right covered in a loopy, extravagant script. A name stuck out in the middle of the page. His name.

He started reading, and before he knew it, he'd sat down in that straight-backed chair.

THE DOORMAN RANG just as Holly was attempting to put a string of lights over the kitchen door. She teetered on the chair, Ellen's gasp from behind her making things much worse. The lights tumbled, landing on the floor with a suspicious splat, but Holly got down safely.

Ellen was already at the intercom. "It's the Christmas tree," she said, her voice as excited as a child's.

A masculine cough came out of the speaker. "You want I should send them up?"

"Yes. Of course."

Ellen lifted her finger from the button and gave Holly a broad grin. "I've worked here four years. He's never once had a tree. Or any decorations at all."

"Do you think he'll be mad at me?"

"Probably. But who cares? It's Christmas."

"Damn straight." Holly turned to reassess the space they'd chosen for the tree. It was near the big window, behind the couch. The lighting wasn't the best there, but that would make the lights on the tree seem all the brighter.

She wished they had more ornaments. But Ellen was able to pick up only so much on her outing today. Maybe tonight, after dinner, Holly could convince Charley to do a little shopping. Walking down Park Avenue at Christmas was always wonderful. With Charley, it would be a slice of heaven.

Loud boots in the hallway announced the delivery

men before they knocked. Holly flung the door open, desperate to see her tree.

But all she saw was a big, tied-up bundle. She pointed to the corner. "Over there," she said.

"Did you bring the stand?" Ellen asked.

"Got everything you'll need except the trimmings."

"Very good."

She and Holly followed them as they traipsed through the living room. The thumps she'd heard outside must have been them cleaning off the muck from the street, because not one of the three men left a mark.

They worked quickly, with very little discussion as men do when they've been doing a job for a long time. And yet there was something lovely in their synchronicity. All three were large men, muscular, and they used their strength impressively. In fifteen minutes, the stand had been erected over a large tarp, the tree had been fitted and straightened, and the tree skirt slung around it. All that was left was to cut the rope holding the branches.

Holly was nearly dancing in her excitement, still awed by the sheer height of the Douglas fir. Charley was going to love it.

Gary, the biggest of the men, and the oldest, took out a pair of shears that could have cut the Verrazano Bridge in half. "Stand back," he said, and they did.

The shears cut through the thick rope like paper, and in a terribly anticlimactic move, the ropes fell to the floor. The branches sagged. They didn't look festive as much as resigned.

By the time she was over her disappointment, Holly realized the delivery men were at the door, and Ellen was handing them some money. Holly should have given the tip, but she was low on cash. She must remember to go to the bank in the next day or so.

"Ellen, you did wonderfully. It's gorgeous."

"Wait an hour. The branches will have all spread out by then."

"You realize we don't have nearly enough ornaments."

"You still have a few days till Christmas."

"You're right. Charley and I will have to get busy."

Ellen shook her head and studied Holly with pale blue eyes. Holly couldn't guess her age. Fifty? Sixty? A slender woman with wiry arms, she was strong, sure on her feet. She didn't take any nonsense from anyone. Holly liked her a great deal.

"I can't get over it." Ellen smiled again, as if at a private joke. "You call him Charley."

"Of course."

"No matter what, you keep after him, you hear me?"

"Keep after him about what?"

Ellen got busy picking up some stray fir needles, but Holly detected a bit of color on her cheeks.

"Come on, Ellen. Tell me what you mean."

The older woman stood, placing the flat of her hand on her lower back. "All I'm sayin' is that you're good for him. Just what the doctor ordered. So you keep after him to make things right."

"He's the one who found me."

Ellen nodded. "That's all I'm sayin'." She looked at the needles in her hand, then at her watch. "Oh, lordy, I'm gonna be late for my bus."

"Is there anything I can do?"

"Just get out of my way."

Holly did. Ellen marched into the kitchen and came out several seconds later dressed in her heavy coat, galoshes and thick gloves. She wore her purse over her coat, the strap from shoulder to waist, the purse itself over her tummy. No one was going to mug her.

Holly closed her eyes at a sudden pain in her forehead. Mugged. Had she been mugged? Had she been careless with her purse and...

She had no purse. No money. No identification. Everything she'd bought yesterday had been with Charley's money, not her own.

The dizziness came back, that sinking-into-a-pit feeling that made her grasp the back of the couch.

"You all right, honey?"

Holly nodded, but slowly. "I'm fine. Just too much excitement, I guess."

Ellen wrapped her hands around her purse strap and started to take it off. "I can catch the next bus."

"No. No, please. Don't. Go get your bus. You've been too kind to me already. I'll feel horrible if you have to stay late."

"But if you aren't feeling well..."

"Charley will be home any minute. I'll be fine. I promise." She let go of the couch and realized she hadn't been lying. "Really. It was just a momentary dizzy spell. I'm perfectly okay."

Ellen gave her a once-over, then nodded. "You go get yourself a snack. Some protein. Maybe a glass of milk."

"I will," Holly said, walking Ellen to the door. "You

just get home safely and have a lovely night with Bert and Chery."

"I intend to. I'll see you in the morning."

Holly planted a little kiss on the woman's cheek. Ellen laughed as she walked out the door. Holly listened to the wonderful sound until the elevator door closed.

She had a lot to do before Charley came home, not the least of which was take a shower. After all the decorating this afternoon, she was a mess.

One last look at the tree bolstered her excitement. The branches were spreading nicely. She headed for Charley's room, stopping at the door.

This was where she'd worked most of the afternoon. His room had gone from utilitarian to sparkly wonderland. She'd decorated everything she could reach. When she turned the overhead lights off and turned hers on, the place came alive with color and movement and Christmas spirit.

All the while she decorated, she'd kept wondering what it would be like to make love in a room like this. To sink into the color and light as if it were six feet of snow.

Maybe they'd find out. If she could convince Charley that while waiting for the wedding night was sweet and romantic in theory, it pretty much sucked in real life.

She flung the closet doors open, her gaze going straight to the stack of new hangers Ellen had brought home from her shopping trip. That's what Holly should have done first, before the decorations. Oh, the heck with it. What's a wrinkle among friends?

She chose a little black dress for tonight. She wanted the room to shine, not her.

Holding her dress in one hand, she closed the closet door, but she didn't rush off down the hall. What she wanted to do was take a bath in Charley's tub. It was gigantic, and it had all these jets all over the place, and she'd been thinking about it all day, in between her very X-rated thoughts about the bed.

Who was she kidding? She wanted him. She wanted him bad.

What the heck. She made one quick trip to the guest room, but only to get undergarments. Then she hurried back and walked into the largest bathroom she'd ever seen.

White tile dotted with the most beautiful throw rugs made for an interesting contrast that was echoed throughout the room. The smooth glass of the mirrors was offset by the granite of the sinks. The towels were thicker than her winter coat, pure white, divine. There was nothing on the counters. Not even the usual stuff like toothpaste or a hair dryer. None of that mattered when she saw it: the tub built for two dozen of her closets friends. Well, maybe not that many. Actually, two would be just right. Cozy, but not cramped.

She turned on the water, waited a moment till she got the temperature right, then she took her clothes off. Before the tub was even half-full, she got in. It seemed bigger than ever.

There was an electrical console behind her and she wondered about the safety, but then figured there was no way Charley would have anything but the absolute best in his penthouse. So she read the dials. Several of them controlled the jets in the tub, another piped in music, there was an intercom that connected to several rooms and to the intercom from downstairs. Oh, heavens, there was even a phone.

The water had filled up to her breasts, and she actually had to hang on to the bars on the side of the tub to keep from floating. She turned off the tap, then faced the console. Music first, even though she was dying to get to the jets.

A very soothing, light classical station came on. She wouldn't change that. She hit the first jet and the tub sprang to life. By the time she'd finished pushing buttons and turning dials, she'd been transported to some other place. Her body's every need, except one, was being tended to, massaging away more aches and pains than she'd realized she had. The sound of the bubbles mingled with "Clair de Lune," and she found the pièce de résistance—a soft headrest behind a big bottle of bath oil.

She adjusted it under her neck, then closed her eyes. She was never leaving here. Never. The only thing that could make it more perfect was if Charley was in here with her.

How had she gotten so lucky? She must have done something wonderful in a past life.

At the thought, an image came to her of a Christmas tree. Not the one in the living room. This one wasn't big and fresh and deep green. In fact, it looked old and crooked, and it had very few needles left. It was better for burning than for displaying the pathetic little ornaments. The vision, very vivid, brought her down, she couldn't say why. She just felt badly for the poor lady who had to settle for that tree, when Holly had gotten the pick of the forest.

With a little shake of her head, she banished the sadness. This was a time to relax and enjoy, to be swept away by sensation and sensuousness.

But the picture in her head didn't disappear entirely. A small fragment, a shiny picture hung from an almost bare limb, niggled at her. She couldn't make out the picture, though, and finally the water had its way with her and the image floated away.

12

THE FIRST THING HE SAW was the tree. The scent of
Douglas fir took him back to his childhood, to the excitement leading up to Christmas Day. His mother had
been extravagant with Christmas, decorating anything
she could get her hands on. His father had been less interested: he basically just showed up when expected.

There had been a time in Charles's life when Christmas had meant nothing but pleasure. The cook had
gone overboard with all manner of cookies, and most
years he'd eaten them until they'd hidden the cookie
jar. Music had filled the house, mostly Johnny Mathis
and Nat King Cole. The presents would start appear-
ing a week before they were to be opened, with the
bulk of them showing up on Christmas morning.

They tended toward books and clothes, but every
year he got something grand and special. A bike. A
telescope.

He hadn't thought about any of this for a long time,
except to dismiss the random recollections. Like his father, Charles had grown less interested in the holiday
as he'd gotten older, but now he wondered if his blasé
attitude could be attributed to something besides
work.

Great. Jane had been in his life for two days, and already he was thinking about going to a psychiatrist. It

wouldn't be David, that was for sure. The man knew enough of his secrets.

Charles hung his coat and stuffed his gloves in the pockets. It was very quiet, and that made him nervous. He'd expected Jane at the door, wearing something scandalous. Ellen had clearly gone home, and now that he took a good look at the living room he could see lights strung crookedly along the door frames and cornices. Jane had been a busy girl.

He headed for the back of the apartment, sure he'd find her standing on something precarious, reaching to string more lights. Taking chances again, even with the fresh bruise on her head. Although he wasn't crazy about it, he'd help her. He didn't want her breaking her neck.

As he approached the bedroom, excitement built in his chest, in his arms. He wanted to see her. There was no denying it. He'd learned a great deal this afternoon. Not as much as he could have. As soon as he'd realized what he was doing—that he was reading something so private—he'd slammed the journal closed, but what he had read had shocked the hell out of him.

Jane had been in love with him for a long time, ever since she'd come to work for him. Why, he had no idea. He'd never been nice to her, or attentive. In fact, he felt embarrassed about his attitude toward her. He could certainly be a callous bastard.

It was ridiculous, really. She hadn't been in love with him so much as she had been infatuated with the idea of him. The man she'd written about was kinder, smarter, stronger, handsomer than Charles would ever be. And yet there were some truths. Some insights that had taken him aback.

Jane wasn't someone to be dismissed. He'd seen intelligence, wisdom, acute observations. She made him laugh. But even with such sterling attributes, Jane had hidden behind a cloak of ordinariness.

He hadn't read enough to understand her fully, but he felt certain her problems had come from being sister to Felicity, Pru and Darra. The poor girl had been overshadowed at every turn.

The crack on her head had done more than given her a bruise. It had exposed the person Jane was supposed to have been, only Jane didn't know it.

He started down the hall toward the guest room, but his door was closed. What would he find on the other side? The possibilities were staggering. Endless. He turned the knob and opened the door.

His mouth dropped at the millions of lights, most of them blinking—blue, red, green, white, purple—all of them glittering in the otherwise dark room.

Holly wasn't in the bed, and he made his way toward the closet as he tried to compute that this circus tent had once been his tidy oasis from a busy world.

She wasn't hiding in the closet.

If she was here, and he couldn't believe she would have left, it meant she was in the bathroom. He stood before the door, wondering what he ought to do.

She was most likely decorating in there, although there was a chance she was doing something far more mundane. A knock was most certainly in order.

His knuckles hardly made a sound. He cocked his head and listened for her voice. The lights distracted

him and he closed his eyes, listening harder. Nothing.
He knocked again.

"Charley?"

"Yes."

"Come in."

"Are you decent?"

"Of course."

Even with her assurance, he hesitated. Oh, he
wanted to see her. That wasn't what made him pause.
It was what he was going to want to do to her that cre-
ated the real problem.

Slowly, he turned the knob and walked into the
bathroom. The lights had been turned off, but the space
had a hazy glow. Candles. In fact, the utility candles he
kept under the sink.

Music. Classical. "Moonlight Sonata."

And to top it off, the scent of roses.

"Hey."

He walked the last few paces and saw her in the tub.
Not surprisingly, she wasn't decent. She hadn't even
bothered with soap bubbles or water jets.

She lay in the tub naked, beautiful, sinfully inviting.
Her curls cascaded around her head on a pillow he
didn't recognize. Her right hand dangled over the edge
of the tub. The lighting wasn't good enough to see the
details, and for that he was grateful. Because he was in
enough trouble as it was.

To say he got aroused would be a criminal understatement. He pressed against his trousers in a most
uncomfortable way, and the steam from the bathwater
seeped under his clothes, making him itch to tear them
off.

"Well?" she asked, her voice as sultry as the air. "What do you think?"

He said something. It sounded like, "Abawah."

She smiled. "I see."

"You're..."

"It's called bathing."

"But—"

"Charley?"

He nodded, growing stupider by the second as all the blood that should have worked his brain rushed south.

"Come here."

He took a tentative step.

She shook her head. Her skin shimmered with pearly drops of perspiration.

He was suddenly thirsty. Completely lacking in any kind of moisture whatsoever. He wanted a drink. He wanted her.

She raised her right hand and crooked her finger, motioning him to come closer.

Another step. He was almost at the side of the tub. He could see her better now, the candlelight's shadows dancing on her bare body. God, she was incredible. Round where she should be round, full, ripe, ready. He had to leave before something dreadful happened. Before he had no working brain cells left.

"Closer," she whispered.

He leaned forward, obeying her even when he knew that she was dangerous. That with every second, her power over him grew.

"Not close enough."

He leaned over her, barely steady enough not to put

a bracing hand on the wall. Inches from her lips, he understood now that she'd wanted a kiss. Okay. He could do that without disgracing himself. At least, he hoped so.

She parted her lips, and then he felt her hand on his tie, tugging him closer. But instead of the kiss he'd prepared for, she licked his lips as if he were an ice-cream cone, then pulled, hard, on his tie.

The hand that should have saved him rose too late. Instead of the wall, it went right into the water. Despite her delighted laugh, she wasn't satisfied with that, and while he struggled to get up, she yanked him down.

She might be a tiny thing, and he might be able to best her at arm wrestling with both hands tied behind his back, but he fell. Fell with a wicked splash, in his suit, in his shoes. Fell into the warm water and into her arms.

He knew he'd made a horrible mess, but he didn't give a damn. Not after she gave him the kiss she'd promised. Not when she'd placed his hand on the warm, wet pillow of her breast.

He pulled away from her lips, a moment of sanity sending out great neon warnings. "What in hell are you doing?"

"It was an accident. Although now that I think about it, you did look like you needed a bath."

"My clothes are ruined."

"Who cares about clothes?"

"My shoes are Italian leather, handmade by a little old man in Tuscany."

"I don't care if they were made by Geppetto. They're

only shoes. So are you going to kiss me? Or are we going to talk fashion?''

He captured her lips.

And then he surrendered.

Her tongue slipped between his teeth, and for a long time that's all they did. Kiss. Not just kiss. They made out like teenagers, greedily, hungrily, tasting everything, wanting more.

His palm on her nipple, the stiff bud the only thing in the universe that could have shared his attention, tested his resolve.

Just as he decided to turn to the morsel under his hand, she pulled back. Her smile worried him. A lot.

"Stand up."

"What?"

"Do it. I'll help. Grab the bar there. Go on. Just put your feet on either side of me."

Inexplicably, he did. Somehow, he managed to get to his feet. He dripped from everything. His discomfort had reached an all-time high, and yet he didn't leave. He didn't even move.

Holly grabbed the bars on either side of the tub and pulled herself up until she stood in front of him. His hands went to her waist, but she stopped him and put them back down at his side. "You just stand still," she said, "until I tell you to move."

The first thing she did was twirl her index finger, letting him know he was to turn around. He did. Then she hefted his jacket off his shoulders, down his arms. Threw the sopping mess onto the floor by the tub. Next, she twirled him back to attend to his tie. It wasn't an easy job to get it loose in its current state. His cuff

links proved even more difficult, but once they were
conquered, his shirt came off with nary a whimper.

It felt decidedly peculiar to be knee-deep in water, in
his shoes and socks and pants. Not terrible, really.
Odd. He tried to imagine anyone in his life—David,
Mrs. Robinson, Ellen—walking in on him. Of course, if
David walked in, he wouldn't notice anything amiss,
he'd be so taken with Holly, but the women would
probably die of shock. Huh. The most predictable man
on the East Coast wasn't quite so predictable now.

Holly's hand went to his belt buckle, and he got predictable in two hot seconds. Like any normal, hetero-
sexual, sex-starved man, he groaned as her fingers
pulled and pushed the leather, moaned as she found
his zipper, and turned into a babbling idiot as the zipper started down.

"Hmm," Holly said, stopping the progress after
about an inch.

"*What?*"

"I was just thinking—"

"Think later."

"But—"

His hands went to her arms as he lowered his gaze to
hers. Never had words come so hard. Never had he
been so hard. But it had to be said. "Holly. This isn't a
good idea. I think you'd better leave now."

"What? I didn't understand a word you said."

Okay, so he'd have to unclench his jaw. "I think
you'd better leave."

"Now?"

He nodded.

"Why?"

Despite the ease with which it would communicate the irony of her question, he couldn't get his brow up. It was the only thing he couldn't get up, however, and the clock, as they say, was ticking. "Just go."

"I don't want to. I like it in here. Besides, I'm not finished."

"If you touch me one more time, I won't be able to stop. Do you understand?"

"Yes."

"So why aren't you leaving?"

"For one thing, if you hold me any tighter I'm going to lose all the feeling in my hands. And for another thing, I don't want to leave. I want to see you."

"I'm right here."

"I want to see you naked."

"Abawah."

"What does that mean? You've used it twice now."

He shook his head, trying to will her away. Trying to will her to stay.

Her hands went back to the zipper and she grasped the little silver tab. Knowing full well she was killing him, she continued to pull it down. He hadn't known she was this cruel, but there was definitely an evil glint in her eye.

He needed this to stop. *Now.* Well, okay. Really soon.

She got the zipper all the way open, and then she slid down into the water until she was kneeling. He heard soft, hysterical laughter, and realized it was coming from him. Holly didn't seem to be having any trouble. She wrapped her fingers around his pants and tugged.

A moment later, he felt cool air on his wet—

"Oh, mama," she said.

They were the most reassuring two words he'd ever heard.

"And you wanted to wait for the wedding. What were you thinking?"

"I have no idea."

She dropped her grip on his pants and they splashed down in the water. It was a most undignified situation. He should do something about that. He wasn't the kind of man to stand paralyzed with his trousers around his ankles. He liked to think of himself as dashing. A roué. A rake.

All he was right now was putty in her hands. So to speak.

She touched him. His eyes rolled up and his lids closed. She flicked her tongue like a little snake. He had to grab the towel rod.

She took him into her mouth.

He understood all there was to know about paradise. Well, almost.

13

HOLLY FELT HIS HANDS on her arms, felt the tug as he pulled her to her feet. She didn't want to stop yet. She'd only had that tiny taste. More. She wanted so much more.

Her gaze moved up his body, past the flat, corded stomach with the frown of a belly button, then the broadening V from his hips to his shoulders. As he lifted her slowly upward she couldn't resist licking his damp skin, clean and slightly salty, from the base of his ribs most of the way up his chest until she couldn't reach it anymore.

She'd been limp in his arms, but now she found her feet and she stood on her own. He let go, but not for long. His hand went to her hair, his fingers slipping through her curls, and he tugged her head back, exposing her neck, making her unbearably aware of her naked flesh.

He kissed her. Despite the frenzy she could feel just under his skin, he took his time. He took possession of her, her mouth, her body, her soul. He had her, and she would have done anything on earth to please him.

He moved from her mouth to her neck, licking, nipping the tender skin, and when he reached the hollow spot, he swirled his tongue in a way that made her squeeze her legs together.

"Step out of the tub," he said, his voice thick with desire.

She obeyed, shivering a little. While she waited, he untangled his clothing and removed his shoes so that when he joined her on the white tile he was gloriously naked.

Reaching behind her, he pulled a thick, white towel from the rack. It went around her like a shroud, covering her from shoulders to just above her knees. His hands moved down her back as he dried her, but the towel was between them, and that wouldn't do.

Grasping the edges of the terry cloth, she opened her arms wide and stepped closer to him, wrapping herself around his waist. As he continued his methodical massage, she rested her cheek against his chest. His heartbeat melded with the sound of violins. She inhaled his scent as if it were the rarest spice.

He moved in such a way that his thick erection pressed against the base of her tummy, and if she could have climbed the man she would have. "Charley?"

"Hmm?"

"You don't have to dry me."

"I don't?"

She shook her head, rolling her cheek against his heated flesh. "I want you inside me."

"I know," he whispered.

He stopped rubbing her back, and his hands went to her arms once again. This time, he maneuvered her so that she leaned against the bathroom wall. He kissed her gently, just lips on lips. "Holly, we can stop now. We need to stop now."

"Why?"

He didn't look at her. She raised his chin with her fingers until their gazes met.

"Why?"

"Because I— It's too soon."

"Too soon? I've loved you forever."

"I think I believe you."

"You should."

"But—"

"I've dreamed of you night after night. You've been in every fantasy I've ever had, and you've been delicious in them, but I don't want fantasy anymore. I want you. I want you inside me. I want to taste every part of you and I want to watch you when you climax, and I want you to lie in my arms when you have nothing left inside you."

"Stop. It's more complicated than that."

"No it isn't."

"There are reasons."

She rose on tiptoe and kissed his protests away. "There's only one reason we found each other again, Charley. Only one. Because we're meant to be together. Don't you see? It's fate, and it's destiny, and it's everything right and good and important."

His dark-chocolate eyes explored her face as if seeing her for the first time. The confusion was all there in the furrow of his brow, the contraction of his jaw muscle. What she didn't understand was why he was so determined not to make love, when it was so very obvious they both wanted to. It didn't make sense.

She shifted the towel on her shoulder to free her hand. When she caressed his cheek, he closed his eyes and pressed against her. "I know you wanted to wait until the wedding, but I've got news for you, big guy. I'm already yours in every way that matters. I love you. I see you. Not just what I want to see, either. All of you. We're supposed to be together. We're better when we're together. Don't you feel it?''

He stilled her hand with his. For a long moment all she heard was the cello coming from the radio, a mournful sound, almost weeping. All she saw was the desire and uncertainty in his eyes.

"I do feel it," he whispered. "I want you more than I've ever wanted anything. But I also know that there are consequences to our actions. That sometimes wanting isn't enough."

Her heart stopped. "What are you saying?"

He let go of her hand. "You'd better get dressed. You'll catch a cold."

She exhaled, hardly realizing she'd held her breath until she felt light-headed. A flash of sparkly lights danced around the perimeter of her vision.

"Holly?"

She tried to speak to him, but she couldn't. Her hand went out to grasp something, to keep herself steady, but before she could find purchase she was in his arms and halfway to the bedroom door.

Scared, not at all sure what was going on, she rested her head against him, grateful for the comfort of his strength. What was happening? It didn't feel like a case of disappointment. It felt as if something was wrong inside her. Terribly wrong.

He laid her down on the bed, and it took her a moment to realize the flashing lights, the waves of color, were real—the decorations from this afternoon. Even when she closed her eyes, she could still feel the pulse of the lights, and oddly enough, the sensation comforted her.

"I'll stop these damn things," he said, pushing off the bed.

She caught him at the last second. "Wait."

"You went so pale. I thought you were going to pass out."

"I think I was. But I'm not now. And the lights feel good."

He looked at her crookedly. "Are you sure?"

She nodded, then tugged at his arm. "Sit with me."

"I'd better put something on."

"If you want to. But don't worry. I won't take advantage."

"I'm not worried about *you*."

"Liar."

He smiled, and she felt whole and fine once more. After moving her leg a bit to the right, he sat down on the edge of the bed. "What was all that about?"

"I'm not sure. I think I got the vapors."

"The vapors?"

She nodded. "Either that, or I grew faint with frustration."

"Right."

"Now, it could happen. I mean, you really did spoil the party."

"Is it so bad to wait?"

She knew he wanted an honest answer. Looking at him, still naked as the day he was born, so beautiful she ached to climb right onto his lap and sit there for a week, she could see he needed her agreement. Even though she disagreed quite vehemently. "It's not *so* bad."

"It's not that I don't want to—"

"I know. I mean, I kind of had some physical evidence, if you get my drift."

He cleared his throat, but she detected a hint of a grin. "I do."

"It could have been fantastic."

"I know that, too."

"Well then, I have a question for you."

"Shoot."

"What if we, um, did some other stuff."

"Other stuff?"

She punched him in the shoulder.

"Oh, you mean *that* kind of other stuff."

"We wouldn't be the first."

He nodded, as if contemplating a business merger. "And I suppose we wouldn't be the last."

She scooted up the bed a bit, until her head was comfortably on the pillow. Suddenly, she felt naked again. Not just undressed. "Actually, the more I think about it, it's probably the best thing we could do."

"Your reason being..."

"For one thing, there's the whole compatibility issue."

"Are you saying there might be a chance I wouldn't like making love with you?"

"No. But I might not be so crazy about you."

His eyes widened in horror. "You take that back."

"Nope. I think you have some proving to do, buddy. I mean, you're the one who asked me back, not the other way around."

"I'm beginning to regret that."

"No, you're not. You love me being here. Admit it."

Another slow smile changed his face. "I don't hate it."

"Boy, talk about not giving an inch."

He looked down. "I intend to give a lot more than an inch. Just not today."

She laughed. "Rest easy, cowboy. I've seen ample evidence that you're, well, ample."

He rolled his eyes, then narrowed his gaze on her once again. "Uh, speaking of evidence, what's with all the lights?"

"It's Christmas."

"That's what I thought. So why are we sitting in the middle of a Las Vegas showroom?"

"You don't like it?"

"Don't pout. I didn't say that. It's certainly... colorful."

"It's artistic." They both looked up at the ceiling, where she'd arranged a gaggle of red lights to spell out the word *joy*.

"Artistic."

"Yes. Very. It's wonderful, and you know it. You just don't like change, that's all."

"You've got me there. I do not like change."

She propped herself up on one elbow, grabbed him around the neck and pulled him down. "Get over it," she whispered. And then she kissed him.

Charles felt himself falling. Falling into the softness of her mouth, falling to the bed, falling...

The way she kissed him, so hungry and wild, made him hard again. Before he touched her breasts, before he let himself think about what he was doing, he was a goner. Her beauty had defeated his defenses. Her warmth and willingness, her scent, the very way she breathed, shredded the last of his good sense.

He wanted nothing else in this world than to be with this woman.

Shifting, but not letting go of her lips, he lay beside her, both of them naked and mostly dry amid the brilliant lights. Surreal, and yet perfect. She deserved a million lights.

Her other hand went to his back to hold him steady as her body arched in its eager readiness. He found the hard nub of her nipple and squeezed it gently between his thumb and finger. Holly gasped, breaking the kiss, and though he was torn, he had to move down and take her exquisite bud in his mouth. He teased her, swirling his tongue until she arched again.

The swell of her hip nudged his thigh, and even there her skin excited him, made him feel domineering and protective all at once. She was so delicate, this exquisite creature in his bed, and yet he knew she didn't want him to hold back.

As he sucked her nipple sharply, his free hand moved down her body, over the silken valley of her stomach, until his fingers touched the patch of curls that hid the most intimate of her secrets. He touched them for a moment, marveling at how she was so different from him in so many ways.

She arched again, this time with her pelvis. "Charley, please."

"Don't be so greedy," he whispered, letting his breath wash over her wet nipple.

"I am greedy," she said. "I want it all."

He felt her hand next to his, and for a moment he thought he might have to fight for position. Instead, she moved with him, both of them reaching down between her legs.

He put his hand on hers, covering it completely, making sure his index finger rested squarely atop her index finger. He looked to catch her eye, but he was distracted by her baby-soft skin and the pouting woman's mouth. "Show me," he whispered.

Her finger moved underneath his, up and down, her stroke slow and measured. His lips closed over her nipple again, and his consciousness was split between the real pleasure on his tongue and his fevered imagination.

He was in a place he'd never dreamed he would be, offered a privileged view. She caressed herself, moving in a way that gave her the most pleasure, teasing herself into a simmer, and he was there for the ride. He wanted to see what her hand was doing, but he couldn't give up his position. Not yet. For now, he let his mind's eye paint the picture.

Her legs opened wider as her finger moved more quickly. He felt her heart rate increase, her pulse quicken, but not in an ordinary way. His skin detected the new rhythms, and his heart and his pulse took up her cadence. Danced to her tune.

But the temptation grew too much for him, and he was forced to let go of her nipple. There was too much to see.

Her eyes were closed, lids fluttering as if she were having the most wonderful dream. Her mouth was open, the thin line of white teeth visible beneath her swollen lips. There was a red flush painting her cheeks, her neck, her chest. That hair of hers, all innocent blond curls, was wild as she thrashed on the pillow.

Her finger had found the right spot, the perfect position. The idea of staying right where he was, as he was, until she took herself to completion was appealing, but it wasn't appealing enough.

He slid down the bed, wondering if she'd noticed the change. He planted tiny kisses along the way, noting places he'd want to explore later, when things weren't quite so urgent.

"Charley?"

He lifted his mouth from just below her navel. "Yes."

"What are you going to do?"

"I haven't decided yet."

She moaned and moved her legs, squeezing them tightly together, capturing her hand in the warm triangle. "Charley?"

"Yes?"

"Please?"

He kissed her again, then continued his journey downward. He understood her simple plea. His answer would come soon. Very soon.

Another kiss, another few inches, and he had to move her hand away. He'd take it from here. He'd take her all the way home.

Using every bit of strength in his body and his mind, he ministered to her in that same slow, deliberate way she'd just taught him. Energy flowed through him as if he were one of the strings of light. His need for release had never been greater, and he wasn't even being touched.

He wouldn't miss a step. First, the long strokes, up and down, tasting her innocence, her heat. Then hardening the tip of his tongue and homing in. Faster now, right there.

Her legs bucked underneath him and he had to hold her hips tight to keep from being tossed off the bed. Her moans grew louder and her head thrashed back and forth, and she kept saying, "Charley, Charley," as her fingers tangled in his hair.

Incredible agony—his need to be in her. Stronger still—his need to give her all the pleasure there was.

Holly stiffened as Charley continued his magic. She felt as if she were outside herself, watching, and here in her body at the same time. This was it. The dream of her life coming true, but better than that. Her dreams had been paltry, she realized now. So small. She'd never realized her heart would swell to bursting, that her breath would stall, then gasp and take in great gulps of his scent and his taste. It was as if she'd looked at a still picture for years, thinking she knew the subject, when all she'd known was the facade.

Charley was making love with her. Charley, who thrilled her with his hands, with his tongue.

No more thought. Just sensation. The way he made the tip of his tongue so sharp and hard, the way he knew exactly what to do...

She wasn't going to last long. She tried to tell him, but her words got carried away by moans she couldn't suppress. A spasm from the inside out, her head thrown back, her toes pointed, her hands pulling his hair...

Just as she reached the edge, the very precipice, he stopped. He sat up, lifted her hips in his broad, strong hands, then shoved a pillow under her behind. Then he took her ankles in his hands and lifted her legs until they rested one each on his shoulders.

She opened her eyes to find him staring at her. His face had changed into something feral, something raw and naked and untamed. He pulsed with energy, from the cords on his neck to his rapidly rising chest. Her gaze moved down. He had his hand around his hard length, and as she watched he moved closer to her. He touched her with the smooth warm head and rubbed up and down in the same slow strokes as her hand and his mouth before it.

She struggled, aching to impale herself on him, to make him stop teasing, but he was in control.

Mercifully, he didn't make her wait long. He pushed in, just a little bit. Then his hands went to her ankles, holding her steady.

He thrust inside her in one long stroke. She cried out, grabbed the sheet beneath her and pulled so she could push her hips against his. The way he held her, the way he entered her, took her where she'd never been before. Climbing, soaring, and sweating and pushing, it was inside and outside and it changed everything.

His thrusts grew faster and faster. Her moans and cries louder.

Then, once more, he stopped. He was inside her fully, and she knew he had to be torturously close to his own release, and yet he stopped.

She looked at him. His gaze held her as steady as his hands. More so. He brought her legs down and curled them around his hips. Then, never letting go of her gaze, he rocked forward until he was on top of her, his face level with her own.

"Now," he whispered.

He pulled all the way out of her, then thrust all of him inside her again, and she screamed as spasm after blessed spasm rocked her body. His face contorted into a mask of pleasure and release; his jaw clenched with a cry he couldn't quite hold back.

And he never closed his eyes. He never stopped watching her. He never lost contact.

As she felt his body relax, and her own spasms slowed, he leaned down and kissed her tenderly on the lips.

It was the most perfect moment of her life.

The man she loved loved her back. She knew it with absolute certainty. It was all there in his eyes. He loved her. He needed her. "Destiny," she said, as he lay his head on her shoulder.

"Destiny."

14

ELLEN OPENED THE DOOR, which was exactly what David had hoped for. He needed to speak to her privately before facing Charles and Jane.

"Let me take your coat," Ellen said. "It's freezing out there."

"Thank you." He handed her his coat and gloves. "How are things?"

"I don't know. I haven't seen hide nor hair of either one of them." She looked behind her to make sure the coast was clear, then leaned his way. "The guest room bed hasn't been slept in."

"Really."

She nodded. "And something else. They didn't eat a proper dinner. I found a Brie cheese wrapper on the counter and the crackers were gone."

"Interesting."

"I don't know about this," Ellen said. "I think she's a lovely girl, I really do. And just what he needs. But she's not going to stay Holly forever, is she?"

"No. She won't."

"But she'll remember this, right? She'll remember being with us?"

"I think so, Ellen. But we'll just have to take it one step at a time. Her memories will come back. Maybe slowly, maybe all at once. Either way, we'll be here for her."

"All right, then. How about you get some coffee. I'll go see if I can wake them."

David gave her shoulder a gentle squeeze, then headed for the kitchen. The decorations made him smile. Charles had been living in an undecorated world for so long. This must be breathing life back into him. God, the tree was huge. And unadorned. Something more entertaining must have gone on last night.

He poured himself a mug of coffee, then went to the window in the living room. As he watched Manhattan gear up for the workday, he thought about the research he'd done in the past twenty-four hours. He was utterly convinced Jane would come out of this fine— physically, at least. Nothing in the journals even hinted at anything dire. Emotionally was another subject, and that had more to do with Charles than Jane.

He was so stubborn. The man had been a robot for years, never changing his routine, hardly taking a day off. The company was in excellent shape, and that was all well and good, but Charles had turned into an old man. He needed Jane more than he could ever realize. She was the one person who could break the shackles of his self-imposed exile.

The best thing would be for Jane to slowly remember her past, with Charles there to ease the transition. For both of them to discover a totally new Jane together.

It could happen, if Charles was willing to bend.

"Good morning."

David turned at Jane's voice. She was in a blue silk kimono, her hair tousled from bed, her skin radiant in the morning sun. "You look like you could use some coffee," he stated.

She nodded, then padded toward the kitchen. He could tell she wasn't fully awake. Vulnerable. He followed her.

As she got down her mug, he leaned against the island. "How are you feeling?"

"Tired."

"What about your head?"

She touched the bruise. "It's not so bad."

"I'm glad."

"But..."

"What?"

She poured her coffee, stirred in her sugar substitute, put the spoon in the sink. Only then did she look at him. "But I've been a little dizzy."

"Oh?"

"It's weird. I don't feel sick. Only sometimes things will start to get dark. And it'll feel like I'm falling."

"Why do you suppose that is?"

"The bump?"

"Maybe."

She sipped as she walked, then curled up on the dining room chair with her knee under her chin. "I'm happy. Happier than I've ever been before. It's incredible, really. But there's something else, too."

He sat down opposite her, nodding for her to continue.

"I'm not sure if it's because I've been away, or what. I'm having these dreams, only they're not like any other dreams I've had before."

"About what?"

"An apartment. A Christmas tree."

"You don't recognize them?"

She shook her head. "I don't. And yet they're as clear and detailed as you are right now. I feel as though I can see under the bed, in the cupboards. I kept waking up last night. At least five times. Each time, it was the dream that woke me."

"Want my opinion?"

"Of course."

"I don't think there's a thing to worry about. Whatever the dreams are, you're safe. You're with people who care a great deal about you. Nothing is going to change that."

She gave him a smile filled with secrets. "I do feel safe. Oh, David, it's so good. He's... He's wonderful."

David heard slippers on the tile and turned to find Charles in his bathrobe, looking just as disheveled as Jane.

"He doesn't feel wonderful."

Jane's face lit up at seeing him. And when David looked back at Charles, a similar transformation occurred. Charles was Charley again. The patina of age had disappeared, and his grin had turned devilish. It was a good thing that was happening here. David just wished he could do something to ensure the outcome.

Charley got himself some coffee and joined them at the table. But first, he sidled up to Jane's chair. She leaned her head back. Charley kissed her.

David turned away. It was too intimate a moment for outside observers. All he could think of was that Charley was one lucky son of a bitch.

"I can't believe I'm late again," Charley said as he sat down. "Twice in two days. It's unforgivable."

"Late?" Jane frowned. "You're not going in to work today, are you?"

"What do you mean?"

"Charley, the wedding is in a matter of days. We have a million things to do."

"Oh, no, we don't—" He stopped, looked at David. "We don't have to make a big production of the wedding. I think we should just go to city hall."

"Are you serious?"

He looked back at her. "Yes. I'd rather spend the time with you, if that's all right. No parties, no crowds. Just us."

They were the perfect words. The smile Jane gave Charley was pure satisfaction. "Then that's what we'll do."

"So you'll stay here today? Finish decorating?"

She didn't look so happy about that. "I don't want to stay here all day. I want to go out. I want to go to lunch with you."

Again, Charley gave him a surreptitious glance. David nodded, then masked the move with a sip of coffee.

Charley put his hand over hers. "And where would the lady care to dine?"

"Oh, gosh. I don't know. How about Haute Couture?"

"No!" they both said at once.

Jane's eyes widened.

"The food's not that great," Charley said.

"And it's way overpriced," David added.

"Hmm. I didn't know. How about—"

"I know." David cleared his throat. "I think you should go to Charlemagne."

"It's a wonderful restaurant, but isn't it impossible to get into?"

Charley sighed. "I have a table."

"Goody," Jane said, rubbing her hands together. "And afterward, we can go pick up the decorations for the tree."

"I can't be gone that—"

David kicked Charley in the shin.

"Ouch."

Jane frowned. "What's wrong?"

"The coffee was too hot." David gave Charley a raised brow. "He'd love to go with you. You two can have a great day on the town."

Charley wasn't happy about this pronouncement, that was clear, but he only glared at David. When he turned to Jane he was all graciousness. "That's right."

Jane uncurled her legs and stood. "Then hurry up. Go to work. I want to have lunch early."

Charley frowned. "How early?"

"Ten?"

He shook his head.

"Eleven."

"Nope."

"A quarter to twelve."

He stared at her for a long moment. "A quarter to twelve it is."

She rewarded him with a kiss. Charley's hand went to the back of her head to hold her steady. It wasn't a big move, but it was significant.

David sighed. It was all going to work out. No doubt about it.

CHARLES HUNG UP his cell phone and put it in his briefcase. He stared at David, not really seeing him, thinking through the information he'd just received from Sterling. While he'd been playing house with Holly, Riverside had gone over to Trump, and the two of them had agreed to purchase the land surrounding the industrial complex. That wouldn't have been a problem, except that it looked as if they were going to get the zoning changed. Someone had greased some palms while Charles had been sleeping, and as it stood right now, Warren Industries could lose millions.

"What was that all about?" David asked.

"A business deal has gone badly."

"That's a shame. But I'm sure you'll fix it."

Charles shook his head, then stared out the car window at too many vehicles trying to fit into too small a space. "I've dropped the ball, David."

"Two days? You're going to begrudge yourself that?"

"Two days is all that's necessary. I didn't pay attention, and it's the stockholders who are going to pay."

"I hate to say this, as I know it's a sore subject, but why the hell are you the only one in that company who could have handled this?"

"The name of the company should give you a clue."

"Don't give me that. You have some excellent people working for you, Charley, and you don't let them do their jobs. So you have no life, and they have no pride. Sonia Anderson. There's a perfect example. She's a hell of a smart woman who could probably save you a few million if you'd listen to her, but you don't. It's you or it's nobody. And if something happens to you? It'll be just like when your father died. Except you won't have a son waiting in the wings to take over."

Charles unclenched his teeth. David meant well. But he was no business maven. The man was a doctor, and in all things psychiatric, Charles gave him full credit. But this was his arena, and only he understood the gravity of the situation. "I'll think that over," he said. "But in the meantime, I can't afford to play this little game anymore."

"Game?"

"Look, I've tried to be a nice guy, but I have my limits. You said she'd have her memory back by now. Why doesn't she?"

The look on David's face made Charles wince. "Because we're talking about a human being. A vulnerable human being."

Yes, she was a human being. And a nice one. But when all was said and done, she would go back to her life and he to his. It had been interesting, and last night had been nothing short of miraculous, but Jane was nothing if not complicated. She'd already turned his world upside down. To go on with the charade would spell certain disaster. He wasn't happy about it. But there were consequences. "David, I need you to talk to her. Today. You can meet her at the restaurant. I'm sure if you explain what's going on—"

"What the hell are you talking about?"

"It's over. I'm sorry about that. She's a nice kid. But I can't let her distract me anymore."

David's response was anatomically impossible, yet very succinct.

Charles realized he was going to come out of this the bad guy, even though he felt no ill will toward Holly—Jane. "I'm not telling you to dump her in the middle of Broadway and Fifth, for God's sake. I just think we should help her to get her old life back."

"Is that what you want? For everything to go back the way it was?"

"Of course."

"Then you're a damn fool."

"Thanks."

"I mean it. I love you like my brother, but if you do this, Charley, I don't know what—"

"You won't love me anymore?"

"Stop it, you condescending bastard. You're so above that? You don't need anyone's love?"

Charles checked the address. They were still blocks from the office.

"Charley, listen to me. You need her more than she needs you."

He whirled on David. "What? Are you crazy? I'm not the one with amnesia."

"No? Then why can't you remember what it was like to live your life fully? Why have you forgotten the man you used to be? The man I liked and respected."

"I'm still Charles."

"Well, I don't care much for Charles. I think Charley is a hell of a guy, though."

Charles sighed, wondering how he'd let himself get into this mess. "I never agreed to a life sentence, David. It's time for the charade to end."

"Then you tell her. I'm not going to."

"I can't be gone this afternoon. Didn't you hear what I just said?"

David banged on the window behind Ben. The driver's voice came over the intercom. "Sir?"

"Stop the car, please. I'm getting out."

"David, you can't do this to me. The whole company depends on my being there."

David looked him square in the eye. And then he told Charles exactly what he could do with his company.

When the door had slammed behind David, and Ben had moved back into the flow, if you could call it that, of traffic, Charles's first thought was to call Holly and tell her lunch was off. But halfway through dialing his home phone, he thought about how she'd looked this morning. He'd been awakened by the sun, and he'd been caught by her expression. Her hand had been curled up underneath her chin, her hair tangled around her face, and her eyes had moved behind the lids. She'd been dreaming. And she'd had a smile on her face that had made him ache.

Why the hell had he slept with her? He'd known better. Now it was incredibly complicated, and he had only himself to blame. Damn that Riverside. Charles hadn't trusted him from the start.

Who was he kidding? There was only one person to blame for all of this. Hadn't he learned anything from his father? A wave of anger swept through Charles, an impotent rage that made him wish he was a violent man.

Why? Why had he kissed her? Why had he ever

touched her? And worse, how in hell was he ever going to forget her?

HOLLY KNEW, despite the fact that she was on one of the busiest streets in Manhattan, that the wolf whistle coming from the scaffolding had been for her. She knew this because she kept seeing herself in plate glass windows, and frankly, she was a major hottie. And that was with her coat on.

Wait'll Charley saw her with it off. They might not make it to the store. They'd just have to be creative when they decorated the tree. His old stuffy ties might be just the ticket.

God, it was glorious being outside! Walking down Park Avenue, with the sun shining on her face, the nippy air teasing her cheeks. Everywhere she looked it was Christmas, from the women carrying shopping bags, to the delivery men carting fruit and cheese baskets, to the window displays, to the blue-and-white plastic icicles hanging from the storefront eaves. It was Christmas, but Holly already had her present. The best gift anyone could ever have.

She was in love. And he was in love with her. And they were going to get married, just the two of them, at city hall, and then they were going to fly away on a magic carpet to the most spectacular honeymoon in human history. They might even leave the hotel room.

A businessman bumped her shoulder, then looked at her as if she'd bumped him, but she just smiled and wished him Merry Christmas. Nothing on earth could bring her down from her clouds. Life was so sweet.

She waited with the other pedestrians at the corner,

and as horns honked and taxi drivers cursed, her gaze landed on a little girl standing with her mother. The child, who couldn't have been more than three, was bundled up from head to toe against the cold air. Her little nose poked out of her scarf, pink as a bunny's. The mother, also dressed too warmly in Holly's opinion, smiled at the girl. Oh, my, but she loved her daughter. It was so easy to see.

Was Holly that obvious? Did people look at her and know she was in love? Could they tell that she'd been completely, thoroughly, magnificently ravished?

Her thoughts turned juicy, and she laughed out loud as she thought about last night. And this morning. And again this morning. That Charley! Who'd have thought? The boy had some moves. The way he kissed her and the way he... Well, she'd think about that later. Getting run over by a taxi would sort of defeat the whole purpose. Better she just pay attention to where she was going.

Not only could she not wait to see him, she couldn't wait to tell him her surprise. Fate, her dear friend, had popped into her life this morning in the form of a phone call from Charley's mother. What a dear she was. They'd had a long talk, and Holly had learned a great deal about Charley. About his sense of duty, about his hard work, about the things that made him happy. It was his mother's idea for Holly to make the honeymoon plans. To take care of everything so that all Charley had to do was pack and relax. It was her idea, too, to go to Tahiti, Charley's favorite place in the world.

Now Holly had to decide whether to tell Charley

about the honeymoon today, or to wait and tell him as a Christmas present.

She headed across the street, hugging herself out of sheer joy. Another two blocks and she'd be at the restaurant, and Charley would be there, and there wasn't anything else in the world she needed.

She wanted to get there first to order the champagne. And to make sure her hat fit her just—

Her hand went to her head, but there was no hat. She hadn't worn one. She didn't own one. So why was she—

The darkness crept up on her, and this time the dizziness was more pronounced. She managed to get to the side of the building, to lean on the brick wall, to hold on to a newspaper vending machine.

She hadn't called her mother. That's what was wrong. Her mother was waiting by the phone. How worried she must be. It was inexcusable that she'd forgotten such a thing.

Holly took a deep breath and her vision started to clear. That feeling of blackness faded. The fear didn't. What was wrong with her? Was this going to end up some movie-of-the-week disease tragedy? She finds true love and dies before the last commercial?

No. No universe could be that cruel. People did find happiness. Lasting love. They did; she believed that with every ounce of her being. Why not her? Why not?

Strange about the hat.

She headed back to the center of the sidewalk, letting herself be swept away with the tide of humanity. She searched for a phone and finally found one half a block from the restaurant. But when she put her money in and got the dial tone, the oddest thing happened. She couldn't think who she'd wanted to call. As hard as she tried, she couldn't come up with a name or a face. Not a one.

_____ **15** _____

HOLLY SMILED at the waiter as he refilled her water
glass. She could see from his wristwatch that it was just
past noon. Charley was late. But there was no need to
worry. In a city like this, anything could have happened to delay him. A traffic jam. A phone call. It was
nice and warm here, the waiter didn't seem to mind
that she hadn't ordered yet, so what was the problem?

She took in a deep, cleansing breath and let it out
slowly. If it hadn't been for that dizzy spell, she
wouldn't have given his tardiness a second thought. It
had shaken her; she'd be the first to admit it. Maybe it
wasn't the bump on her head at all. Maybe she had
some sort of virus. A twenty-four-hour bug.

Whatever it was, she wasn't going to let it spoil her
mood.

Her thoughts slipped away into a grass hut with
tropical breezes billowing the curtains. The only thing
they'd be wearing would be wedding rings. Charley
would ask if she wanted anything, anything at all.
She'd tell him she had everything she'd ever wanted.
Then he'd kiss her and the whole universe would be in
his lips and his eyes and the way he touched her just
so.

A little shiver ran through her as she remembered
what it had been like last night, what it would be like

for years to come. How she and Charley would grow old together. How this was just the first of fifty Christmases they'd share....

What had she done last year? Memories darted past, too quick for her to catch. A smell here, an image there, but nothing concrete. No actual memory of Christmas at all.

This was getting scary. Really scary. She must have had a Christmas. She must have been with people she cared about. Right? Or maybe... That was it. Of course. She'd been without Charley. Why would she remember it?

She closed her eyes, picturing his smile. The one that changed his face, that made him young and full of mischief. The smile he shared with so few people. It was one more thing she loved about him—that she got to see the private Charley.

Oh, where was he? She scanned the entryway, but the only newcomers were two elderly women. They did look sweet. Both of them had curly white hair, and they had matching purses. Sisters?

Sisters. Her gaze went to her water glass, but she hardly saw it. She couldn't have said what she was looking at or exactly what she was thinking about. A dream, perhaps, or a movie she'd once seen. Three sisters, each of them more beautiful and talented than the last. For heaven's sake. She shook her head at her own foolishness. Here she was waxing on about a fairy tale! What was wrong with her today?

A laugh from the other side of the restaurant brought her attention back to the room. It was a familiar laugh, one she'd heard many times before. She turned to scan the patrons, but she didn't recognize a soul. The restaurant didn't ring any bells either, now that she thought about it. Except this morning she'd told David she'd been here before.

But surely she would have remembered the rich leather of the seats, the bumpy texture of the wallpaper, the candles on the tables. It was one of the finest restaurants in Manhattan, and according to David, Charley came here at least once a week.

Maybe she'd just seen it on reruns of *America's Rich and Famous*.

She sat quietly, waiting to hear the laugh again. It didn't come. But the waiter did.

"Are you sure you don't want to order?"

"Tea would be nice."

"We have green, pekoe, mint, chamomile, black currant, English breakfast, Earl Gray—"

She held up her hand to stop him. "Goodness. Do you have any regular tea? You know, the kind in the little white bag?"

The waiter gave her a kind smile, not condescending or anything. She'd thought he looked nice, and now she knew she was right. He'd obviously been doing this for years. His red coat looked as though it had seen many a chef, many a customer. "I'll be back in a moment."

"Thank you," she said.

"Oh. Lemon or milk?"

She opened her mouth to answer, but then she realized she wasn't sure. Did she take lemon or milk? It wasn't a difficult question. But no matter how hard she tried, she couldn't remember. It was as if she'd never had tea before.

"I'll bring both, and you can decide then."

He headed off to the kitchen, while Holly tried to get herself under control. Panic swirled inside her like a tornado, threatening to tear her apart. *What was wrong with her?* Why didn't she know anything? And where was Charley?

She couldn't sit here another minute. Not like this. Not when she didn't know how she liked her tea. God, did she have money for a tip? It wouldn't be fair to walk out after he'd been so nice. But maybe she could mail him a tip later.

Her new Prada purse—the one she'd bought this morning—was by her chair, and just as she brought it up to the table, she saw Charley. Relief made her cry out, but she didn't care about the looks from the other tables. He was here. He hadn't forgotten about her.

She trembled in her excitement at seeing him again. He would fix everything. Explain why she was having such a complicated day. She stood, suppressing the urge to run to him. To leap into his arms.

She waited for his smile, the special smile, but when he saw her his lips only curled a bit at the edges. It took her aback, to say the least. This morning he'd made love to her until she'd wept. The look in his gaze had made her feel whole and beautiful and special. When he finally reached the table, she saw it wasn't a trick of the light. "Is something wrong?"

He hesitated as he kissed her on the cheek. "Wrong?"

She took his head between her hands and shifted his

face so she could really see him. But he wouldn't look at her. Not squarely in the eyes. She let go. "Yeah. Wrong."

He sat down, cleared his throat and picked up the menu. He didn't look at it, though. In fact, he opened it once, closed it, then opened it again. "Holly?"

"Hmm?"

He nodded toward her chair. As she sat, she caught two people looking at her—one across the way, and one two tables down. And just like that, the mystery was solved. She should have known better than to expect him to be too affectionate in public. Charley was a private man. She needed to respect that. After all, she had him at night, right?

Charley finally looked at the menu. A moment later, he closed it and shoved it aside.

"Charley?"

"Yes?"

"You seem upset."

"Something happened at work."

"Oh, no. Is everyone all right?"

"Everyone's fine. Only my company's net worth is considerably lower than yesterday."

"Yikes."

He chuckled in that sardonic way he had. "Yikes. I think I'll head up my stockholder's report with that very phrase."

She felt slapped. She'd meant to be sympathetic, and he'd thrown it in her face. If only she was the kind of woman who could hide her embarrassment. She wasn't. Her face burned brighter than the candle on the table.

Charley cursed. "I'm sorry. I didn't mean that."

"Of course you didn't," she said, somewhat molli-fied, more by his tone than the words.

"I was caught off guard today. I didn't follow through on something, and now it's going to cost me big-time. I didn't mean to take out my bad mood on you."

"It's okay. I'm fine. And you will be, too. First, though, let's eat. You can't feel better if your tummy is growling."

He shook his head at her, and presto, the light had returned to his eyes. The affection was there, too. Muted, but that was okay. He loved her. All people in love went through lots of emotions, and it wasn't al-ways buttons and bows.

The waiter came to the table with her tea and asked Charley if he'd like something to drink.

"Scotch, neat."

The waiter winked at Holly, then went off toward the bar. She found herself staring at the tea service. He'd brought a teapot, complete with cozy, a beautiful cup, a bowl with lemon wedges, a small honey pot and a cream pitcher. It was every child's dream of high tea. All she needed were some cucumber sandwiches and tea cakes.

It didn't occur to her until she'd taken a few sips of the delicious tea that she'd mixed it with lemon and honey.

"What's that smile about?"

"Nothing. Just the tea."

"Do you know what you want to eat?"

She nodded. The waiter came back just then and

took their orders. As soon as he was gone, she put her hand on Charley's. "Do you want to talk about it?"

He sighed. "No. I don't. I don't want to spoil lunch."

"Despite the evidence," she said, "I'm not so selfish that I couldn't postpone Christmas decoration shopping until tomorrow. If you need to go back to work, I'll survive."

"I was going to talk to you about that."

"I sorta figured."

"You did, huh?"

"Yep. In fact, if you don't stop clenching your jaw, I'm going to have the waiter put my sandwich in a doggy bag, so you can leave right now."

"How about instead of that we have a nice quiet lunch. Talk a little."

"It's a deal. What do you want to talk about?"

He cleared his throat, which meant he had no idea. The ball was clearly in her court.

"I spoke to your mother this morning."

"You did?"

"She was sorry she missed you. She won at bingo last night. Almost a thousand dollars."

"That's great. What else did she say?"

"She told me about when you were five, how you liked to pretend you were a cowboy. How you ran all over the house riding a broomstick horse."

Charley winced. "I was hoping to keep that special memory under wraps."

"Why? It sounds adorable. I made your mother promise to show me all your baby pictures when she gets home."

"Oh, God."

"Which, you do remember, is the day after tomorrow."

"Pardon?"

"The end of your mother's cruise. She'll be at La Guardia at eight-something. I wrote it all down."

He closed his eyes as if the news was the last straw. But before she could ask him why, the food came: his steak, medium rare, plain baked potato, and her chicken-breast sandwich with lettuce, tomato and mayo on the side.

She got busy preparing her meal, cutting the bread into four small squares, doling out the tomatoes, slicing the chicken. All that was left was the mayo, but she paused in her effort to get it when she caught Charley staring. "What?"

"You do that with everything, don't you?"

She nodded.

"Why?"

She had to think for a moment. And then, of course, she remembered. "It's an odd story, really. Sort of miraculous."

"Oh?"

She nodded. "When I was little I took a sea voyage. In the middle of the Pacific, a great storm blew up and the ship was tossed to bits. I found myself in a lifeboat, alone and frightened half to death. When morning came, I saw there was a small tin of rations in the boat. I had no idea when I'd be rescued, so I was very careful with my food. The habit stuck."

He took a bite of his steak and chewed thoughtfully. After he swallowed, the infamous right brow arched. "A shipwreck?"

"I know. It sounds funny, but it's true."

"Where were you headed?"

She shrugged. "Home."

"From?"

"Away."

"How did you get off your little boat?"

"Oh, I was rescued by a very handsome sea captain. He brought me back safe and sound."

"Really?"

She nodded. "I remember the moon. It was so large. So bright it lit up the sea."

"Who were you traveling with?"

She kept smiling. Even though she didn't have an answer for him. She couldn't remember. Why couldn't she remember?

"Holly?"

A crash startled her, and a second later she realized her teacup had shattered. She didn't remember picking it up, but she must have. Just as she must have had a Christmas before this one.

Charley cursed himself for being the biggest kind of fool. She was losing it. He could see it. Her face had gone white, her eyes dilated. But mostly she just looked terribly lost and afraid. He'd pushed too hard. Too soon.

He waved the busboy away, and he knelt beside Holly and picked up a piece of broken china. But the teacup was forgotten when she looked into his eyes. God, she was so vulnerable. What had he done?

He took her hand in his. "It's all right, baby. Don't worry."

"But—"

"It's okay. It's the bump on your head. It was a little more serious than we thought."

"I've been getting so dizzy. And I don't remember..."

"I know. But I promise, the confusion is going to go away and so are the dizzy spells."

"Are they?"

He rose, put the single piece of china on the table, then leaned over and kissed her gently on the lips. "I promise," he whispered.

When he got back to his seat, she was visibly calmer. Thank goodness. Only, where did this leave him? He liked Jane, he really did. Maybe even more than that. But he couldn't help her. He had his own agenda, and it didn't include someone like her. Jane needed someone to pay attention to her. To be there for the ups and downs. That wasn't him. He couldn't even pay attention to his own life.

But it didn't mean he wanted to hurt her. In fact, he'd pretty much rather jump in front of a subway train than do that. No, she'd gotten to him. It was no use denying that. But he didn't love her. Loving her was a whole different matter.

"Charley?"

"Yes?"

"I was going to wait, but I think I want to tell you now."

"What's that?"

The way she looked at him tore him up. She was absolutely a grown woman, but in so many ways she was a child, too. She needed someone to take care of her.

She leaned forward. "I've gotten our honeymoon."

"Gotten our honeymoon?"

She nodded brightly. "Yes. I've taken care of the whole shebang. Everything. Tickets, reservations, all of it. You won't have to lift a finger."

"But—"

"She asked me not to say, but I have to. Our destination, which I'm not telling you, was your mother's idea. Actually, the whole plan was her idea. Isn't that sweet? I'm already loving her."

"Yes, I imagine you are. And I know she's loving this."

Jane nodded. Her color was back. That was good. And so was her appetite. Damn his mother and her manipulations. Damn David. Why didn't everyone just leave him be? He'd been perfectly happy before all this nonsense, and now look at him.

He should have been back at the office already. He should have told Jane it was over, given her a sympathetic shoulder to cry on and gotten the hell out of Dodge.

But he couldn't tell her, could he? It would crush her, and he couldn't bear that. Some tough businessman, eh? No wonder Riverside had gone over to Trump.

Charles sighed as he watched her nibble her little sandwich. A shipwreck, of all things. He knew it wasn't true, but in an odd way, he liked that she'd come up with something so original. Her imagination intrigued him, even as it exhausted him.

So what's a few more days, eh? It wouldn't do irreparable harm for her to stay, as long as she just stuck to decorating the tree. And to bathtubs.

Oh, damn it, that was the wrong thought. He hardened immediately, just as he did every time he thought of last night and this morning. Thirty-one years old, and he'd finally discovered how incredible making love could be. If only he'd known before, he would have done a great deal more of it. Yeah, right. He must be thinking of some other Charles Warren.

His gaze traveled back to her lips, her eyes. She was dangerous. He wanted her. Now. If he could have, he'd have swept the plates and everything off the table and made love to her right this second. Of course, he'd never be able to come here again, and he really liked the steaks.

"Charley, what's that smile for?"

"I was just thinking about this morning."

"Oh?"

He nodded, feeling his blood stir, his body stiffen.

"The first time, or the second?"

"Both."

"Yeah. Me, too."

He took a bite of steak.

She took a tiny bite of sandwich, then laced her fingers under her chin. "Do you really have to go back to work? I mean, can't things wait till tomorrow?"

"No. They can't wait. But I'm not sure I'd be any good at the office, either. What in hell have you done to me?"

"*Moi?* Nothing. I just added a little spice to your life, that's all. A little pizzazz."

"Pizzazz? Is that what you call it?"

"In mixed company."

He laughed. Although he had no earthly reason to. All he was doing was digging himself a deeper hole.

One that threatened to cave in on top of him. But seeing the laughter in her eyes—

"Charles?"

A female voice came from behind him. Jane looked up and smiled. He turned in his chair as the woman rounded the table.

His smile froze on his face. God, no. Not this. Not her.

"How are you, you sweet thing?" She leaned over and kissed the air beside his cheeks. "I can't believe I found you here. It was just a guess."

"Maybe we can talk later—"

"Talk later?" She waved a copy of *Attitudes* in the air beside her, the cursed ad circled in bright red lipstick. "You brought me all the way back from Europe. I'm not about to wait any longer."

He looked desperately at Jane, willing her to leave, to run. It was as if she was standing in front of a speeding truck and there was nothing he could do about it.

"Aren't you going to introduce me to your friend?"

He got up, spilling his water all over the table. He didn't give a damn. What he had to do was think. Now. Any second it could all come crashing down. "Why don't we have lunch tom—"

The woman, whom he hadn't seen in years, turned to Jane and stuck out her beautifully manicured hand. "I'm Holly Baskin. Who might you be?"

The look on Jane's face would be burned into his mind forever. Panic. Utter, childlike, horrible panic. She looked at him, her eyes brimming with tears. "Charley?" Her voice was high, and so scared.

"I can explain. Really."

"But I don't understand."

"I know. It's confusing, but I swear it'll be all right."

She shook her head. Smiled gamely at Holly. "Excuse me. I have another engagement." She picked up her purse and started to walk away.

Charley reached out for her, but missed her by an inch. "Jane, wait!"

She stopped. Turned to face him. And as she stood between a party of four and an empty table, her memories returned. He could see it in her eyes, in her shoulders, in the trembling of her hand. She remembered who she was, and she remembered what she'd done. With a cry that shattered him like the broken teacup, Jane Dobson turned and ran out of the restaurant.

What in hell had he done?

16

JANE DOBSON. That's who she was, all she was.

She ran out of the restaurant, her eyes so blurred with tears she smashed into a woman getting out of a cab, nearly knocking the poor thing to the ground. "I'm sorry," she mumbled as she veered left down Park. She wanted to disappear, fall off the face of the earth.

Memories bombarded her from all sides. Mother, Pru, Felicity, and of course, Darra. The apartment with its terrible tree. All the pictures of Charles Warren. Damn those pictures and her stupid fantasies.

Why him? Of all the people in the world, the last one she wanted to humiliate herself in front of was Charles Warren.

She bumped her shin on a trash barrel and cried out at the pain and the horror at what she'd done. She'd been naked! They'd had sex. She'd practically raped the man.

She wiped her eyes with the back of her hand, then crossed the street, trying to think what to do, where to go. She knew she must look like a crazy woman from the wide berth she was given on the street. She didn't care, except that if Charles was looking for her she'd stick out like a sore thumb.

There was refuge just a few feet away in a doorway

that looked like it hadn't been used lately. There was no doorman, at any rate, and no overhead light. She backed up into the corner, and for a moment she wondered if her legs were going to give out, but they held.

Then she wept. She cried harder than she'd ever cried, great harsh, burning tears, gasping sobs. She covered her face with her hands, turned toward the wall so no one could see her shame.

It was the essence of a nightmare. The worst possible thing that could happen. How she ever could have thought she was a sophisticated woman-about-town was unfathomable. Laughable. Which was, of course, what he was doing—when he wasn't feeling sorry for her.

Her curse filled the entryway. She was so stupid. What had she been thinking? Something had happened to her—she wasn't sure what—but she did remember the hospital. And something about a plaster statue.

That was the only part of the past few days that was vague. Everything else was crystal clear, remembered in vivid color with every word intact, every touch imprinted forever. She'd kissed him, seduced him, planned their blasted wedding!

After a large sniff, she opened her purse. At least one of her problems was solved—she had tissues. What she didn't have was cab fare. Not even bus fare. Instead she found three quarters, one lipstick and two tickets to Tahiti.

So what now? She could make a phone call, but to whom? Darra was the only one in her family who was in town, and Lord, Jane didn't want to call her. Darra'd never be home, anyway. Or she'd be sleeping. In any event, she'd lend a reluctant hand, then never let Jane forget about it. If she knew the truth of what happened... No. She wasn't calling Darra.

So who did that leave? My God. She had no real friends. Acquaintances? Absolutely. Tons of them. But she couldn't call a one of them now. She'd been living in her little private world, where nothing as base as the truth invaded. Her friends were literary characters mostly, but sometimes movie stars and the occasional rock star. She'd never had room in her life for real human friends. And now she was paying for that in spades.

No way she'd be able to walk to Harlem. Besides, she was freezing. Next time she ran out of a restaurant in a panic, she must remember to take her coat.

She rested her head against the brick of the building. Aside from the humiliation factor, which was growing exponentially as each minute ticked by, she really was in a pickle. She couldn't go back to her job. She had no money except a few dollars hidden in the flour tin. She had no family she cared to deal with, and she had no friends. Loser? Not her. Oh, no.

"Jane?"

She stilled as her name came to her from a distance. Not far, just down the block. Charles. No, no. He couldn't find her. She couldn't bear to let him see her.

Pressing herself into the corner of the entryway, she willed herself small, made herself shrink into the shadows. He walked past her, but he didn't see her. He'd had something in his hand, but she couldn't see what. A few seconds later, she heard her name again. He sounded worried. Probably thought a nutcase like her would do something crazy, like run in front of a cab or walk alone through Central Park at night.

She exhaled, hardly aware that she'd been holding her breath. But then he came into view once more. She froze as he looked at the door right next to her. The thing in his hand was her coat. Again he didn't see her. His gaze moved on, and then he walked on down the street.

She sagged, the last of her spirit carried away by her sigh. She'd been invisible. Just like always. He'd have seen Holly. But her? Heck, she didn't even have on a hat.

She fished out her change from her purse and headed down the street once more, looking for a phone. There was someone she could call. Someone who would help her. David. He'd been kind to her through everything. He'd see her home, and she'd be able to talk to him. He knew the truth already, which was good, because she didn't have the energy for explanations.

There was a phone in the next block. Thank goodness. She was so terribly tired.

CHARLES PACED from the kitchen to the Christmas tree and back again. He'd tried sitting, and that had been a joke. Where was she? How could he have let things get so out of control? He was a damned fool, that's how.

She was out there. Somewhere. Freezing without her coat, confused, scared to death. All because he was so predictable.

He'd gone to Charlemagne twice a week ever since

he'd started at the company. Always the same table, always the same meal. Of course Holly Baskin had found him.

Talk about irony. The moment he'd seen her, he'd remembered why they'd broke up. While she was nice enough, and certainly polished enough, and connected enough, the fact was she bored him silly. The idea of spending the rest of his life with her was absurd.

He looked at the ridiculously large Christmas tree. Holly Baskin would never have bought such a thing. In fact, she would have hired someone to come in and tastefully decorate for the holidays. Nothing garish, certainly no lights in the bedroom.

A week ago, he'd have done her one better by ignoring the holiday completely. His gaze moved to the bedroom. Jane had done things in there, too, that Holly would have never considered.

Holly wouldn't have disrupted his work, wouldn't have distracted him in any way. She'd have done everything right. The right parties, the right charities. Sex on Saturday night, the *Times* on Sunday morning. But wasn't that what he wanted? Hadn't that been the point?

So why did it sound so distasteful? So deadly dull? Damn it. When Jane had run out of that restaurant, his whole world had come to a halt. The thought of losing her for good...

Ellen, who'd had enough sense to stay away from him after he'd given her a brief explanation, came out of the kitchen with a cup in her hand. She handed it to him.

"I'm not thirsty."

"Just drink it."

From the look on her face and the irritability in her voice, he decided it was best to comply. He took a sip and tasted the whiskey lacing the coffee. "Thank you."

"Why did you have to take her to that restaurant?"

"How was I supposed to know Holly would show up?"

Ellen shook her head at him, her eyes accusing him of all manner of crimes. Of course, he'd already condemned himself. "Aren't you going to go after her?"

"I don't know where she is."

"Maybe her apartment?"

"I've called there every ten minutes."

Ellen sighed. "You think she's going to pick up the phone, knowing it's you?"

"Oh."

"I'll call Ben," she said as she headed for the kitchen. The ringing phone stopped her. She looked at Charles. Charles looked back. Then he dove for the phone. "Jane?"

There was no answer, although he heard noises. A scrape, a distant whistle, like from a teakettle.

"I'd like that."

David's voice. Muffled, but definitely David. "Hello?"

"Come on, Jane. Sit down. Finish what you were saying to me."

Charles sagged with relief. Thank God! Jane had obviously called David. They were somewhere—David's apartment, or more likely hers. What he didn't understand was why David wasn't speaking directly to him.

"I just can't believe I'd do that to him, of all people," Jane said, her voice soft, but quite clear.

"Why him, of all people?"

"You know."

"No. I don't. Not really. Not like this."

"Oh, it's so stupid," she said, her voice modulating just enough to make Charles have to strain to hear. "I love him. Even now. Even after I've spoiled everything."

"You love him as Jane?"

"Of course. I have for a long time. Being with him just made things worse. A million times worse. Damn that stupid ad! And damn my stupid imagination." She winced. "Do you know I actually told him I'd been shipwrecked as a child?"

"Pardon?"

"I did. He asked why I eat the stupid way I do. I told him I'd been shipwrecked, that I learned to ration my food from that horrible experience. But you know what? I wasn't. I've never been on a ship in my life, unless you count the Staten Island Ferry. I used to *dream* about being stranded on an island. You know, Brooke Shields and *The Blue Lagoon?* It wasn't my memory. I don't have any memories to speak of. He has to think I'm as crazy as a loon. I have no right to love him!"

"Do you think it's possible he loves you back?"

"Oh, please. David, it's me we're talking about. Not Holly."

"But don't you see, you are Holly."

"I thought I was the one who got knocked senseless by Cupid. I'm not Holly."

"Of course you are. You've always been Holly, but

you've been afraid to show it. And I'll tell you something. If Charley has a brain in his head, he'll see that you're the best thing that ever happened to him. He'll get off his ass and marry you."

Charles winced at David's words, thinking about what he'd almost done. How he'd planned on sending her packing. But marry her? Marry her?

"You're a peach, Dr. David, but you're the one who's in fantasyland now. I saw the real Holly, remember? She is so not me, and I'm so not her."

"I know. And believe me, if you were like her, I wouldn't be having this conversation with you."

Jane said something, but Charles didn't catch it. Her voice grew too soft to hear.

"Charley."

David's voice, loud and clear, startled him. "Yes?"

"Get over here."

"Where?"

"Her apartment, you idiot."

"But—"

"But? *But?* Are you actually going to let her get away? Are you that stupid? Think of it, man. Jane when you go to bed at night. Jane when you wake up."

Charles heard the words. But more than that, he understood them. Jane in his bed. Jane messing up his orderly life. Jane having his children.

"David. Keep her there."

"I'll do my best. But you'd better hurry."

Charles didn't bother saying goodbye. He just hung up and dashed for the door. Ellen was standing at the ready, his coat in her hands.

"Ben is waiting downstairs," she said. "Now, you do the right thing, you hear me?"

"I'll try."

"Don't try. Do it."

He took one second to lean over and kiss her cheek. "I'll be back."

With that, he was out the door and in the waiting elevator. He rocked back and forth as he went down, his pulse revved as if he was getting ready for the starting gun.

Jane. Who would have thought? God, his mother was going to have a field day. And the two of them together? Trouble. Big trouble.

So why the hell was he grinning like a dope?

JANE FINISHED HER TEA and stared at her woeful Christmas tree. It was officially dead now, as it hadn't been watered in days. As dead as her dreams.

Despite what David said, she knew better than to expect a happy ending. Her whole life had taught her that. She wasn't the kind of girl who got the brass ring.

The horrid part was that she remembered everything: how she felt when he kissed her, the way his smile changed his face, how they made love together. Charles might be alive and well, but he was going to haunt her like a ghost for the rest of her life. She'd never forget. Maybe, in time, she wouldn't love him like this. Maybe.

David came out of the bathroom and gave her an encouraging smile. He'd been great. A real friend. Which was something, wasn't it?

"How are you feeling?"

She shrugged. "As well as can be expected."

He put his hand on her shoulder and gave it a reassuring squeeze. "Hang in there, kiddo."

"I'm trying. But I keep thinking about the restaurant, when she walked in waving the magazine around like a handkerchief. Everyone in the place was staring, wondering, I'm sure, who the imposter was. She's everything he should have, David."

"If you don't stop obsessing about this, I'm going to conk you on the head again."

She smiled. "All right. I surrender. I'm not going to obsess. Well, not much."

He frowned.

"Okay. Not at all. I'll be fine. Honestly. I'm sure you have tons of things you should be doing."

"I'm right where I want to be."

She got her bag and pulled out the tickets. "Would you give these to Charles? I'm sure he can get a refund."

David sat down at her little table and opened the ticket jacket. "Tahiti?"

"His mother's idea. She said he loves it there."

"She's right. Have you ever been?"

"Nope."

"Maybe you ought to hang on to these," he said, putting them down on the table.

"It's going to take me a hundred years to pay him back for the clothes. I'll never manage the tickets, too. They're first class."

"I see."

"I bet that's what you say to your patients when you're placating them."

"Ouch. I'm busted."

She kissed him on the cheek. "I know you're the best shrink in the city."

"Only the city?"

She laughed. She hadn't expected to laugh for a long time. "David, I—"

A knock interrupted. She looked at David, then the door. Her heart pounded in her chest, and she found it hard to catch her breath.

"Are you just going to sit there, or are you going to open the door?"

She looked at him again. His expression told her nothing, although there was a certain twinkle in his eye. She stood, telling herself it couldn't be. It was probably the landlord, or Mrs. Erlich from next door. Not Charles. Of course not Charles.

Despite her conviction, she practically ran to the door. She threw it open. And her heart nearly burst.

"Jane," he said. The way he said it was the killer. He said it as if he'd missed her. As if he loved her.

"Charles."

He shook his head. "Charley."

She knew right then it was going to be okay. That she *was* the kind of girl who got the happy ending.

"Are you two just going to stand there all day, or are you going to kiss each other?"

David's words spurred her forward, and Charley, too. She was in his arms, tight against him. His lips on hers in a kiss that was familiar and brand-new. She filled her lungs with his scent, ran her hands down his back. Charley. Charley in her arms.

He pulled back, and she reluctantly let him go. "We need to talk," he said, his voice gruff, the way it had sounded before they'd made love.

She led him into the apartment. David was putting his coat on. "I think it's time for me to leave."

"No, you don't have to."

Charley raised his brow. "Yes, he does."

David sighed. "Ungrateful bastard."

"Go."

He kissed Jane first. Right on the lips. "It couldn't happen to a nicer person. You're incredibly special, you know that?"

She nodded. "I think I do. Thank you."

He let her go, nodded at Charley, and then he was gone and it was just the two of them.

Charley caught her gaze and held it steady. "I'm so sorry."

"You're sorry? I'm the one who spent all your money and moved into your life."

"True. But I still wish it had been easier for you. I never dreamed Holly would show up."

"Oh. Her."

"Don't worry. The minute I saw her I knew I'd made a mistake in placing that ad."

"Really?"

He nodded. "What I didn't understand at the time was that there was someone else for me."

"Someone else?"

He closed the few inches that separated them, then cupped her cheek with his hand. "Someone so beautiful, it makes me ache inside."

She closed her eyes, knowing he was telling her the truth. That in his eyes she was beautiful. And special.

"Jane."

She opened her eyes. "Yes, Charley?"

"I'm in love with you."

"I know. I'm in love with you, too."

"I think we need to do something about it, don't you?"

She nodded.

"I was thinking, maybe we could get married. At city hall. Then fly off to Tahiti. What do you think?"

"I think it's a wonderful idea. In fact, the best idea I've ever heard."

His grin blossomed. "You realize, of course, you've shattered my orderly life beyond all measure."

"Which, in my not so humble opinion, is exactly what you needed."

"When you're right, you're right."

She smiled, but only until he kissed her.

Another knock sounded on the door. Only this time, she really didn't know who it was. "You think David forgot something?"

Charley frowned. "He wouldn't come back. Not if he knew what was good for him."

She headed for the door, dragging Charley with her. She was completely unwilling to let him out of her reach, even for a second.

She opened the door. David wasn't there. But he'd left them a little something.

On her doorstep sat a broken, chipped plaster statue. Cupid.

She sighed as Charley's hand slipped around her waist. "It was destiny all along, wasn't it?"

He nodded, grabbed the cupid, then closed the door.

_____ Epilogue _____

Two months later...

MRS. JANE WARREN squeezed the last of the suntan lotion onto her palm, forming a teetering mound of white goop. Before it all fell in the sand, she bent over Charley and began a long, slow massage on his back.

He moaned and she sighed. There wasn't a happier person on earth right now. There couldn't be.

She was married to the most wonderful, considerate, handsome, sexy...

A deep, almost painful grunt made her ease up on his back. But the distraction lasted only a few seconds. Then she was reliving her wedding, still so fresh in her mind. Five days ago, to be exact, and it had been a stunner.

To say her sisters had been surprised was an understatement. Darra had gotten drunk on champagne and passed out in the coatroom. Guy had gone home with one of the bartenders. Pru had been her usual melodramatic self, incensed that she hadn't been invited to play the wedding march. Jane had tried to explain it wasn't that kind of wedding, but Pru wouldn't listen. Felicity had been a peach, though. After the initial shock, that is. It had been fun to bring her family together without them knowing what for. Her mother was furious with her, but she'd get over it.

They'd all had a wonderful time. Everyone danced until the wee hours of the morning, drank too much, laughed too much, and generally caused havoc all over the Westminster Regent.

The honeymoon had been glorious so far. Two days of lolling in bed, floating in the remarkable blue of the Tahitian ocean, sipping fruity cocktails and soaking up the sun. Two nights of the hottest sex this side of—

"Oh, right there." Charley moaned and she focused on her hands. He'd go see the real masseuse this afternoon, but she still wanted to do what she could to relax him. Poor baby still took himself too seriously. She pressed her palms down harder. "Charley?"

"Hmm?"

"You know what I was thinking?"

"Hmm?"

"It would be most excellent if we made a baby this week."

His muscles tensed beneath her hands, then a second later he rolled over onto his back. "A baby?"

She nodded. "Why not?"

"We've only been married five days."

"So, you want to wait?"

He nodded as he took her shoulders and pulled her down on top of him. "Not forever," he said, once he'd captured her gaze. "But there are things I want to do first."

"Such as?"

"Ravish you. Make you happy. And find out everything there is to know about you."

"Everything?"

"Maybe not. But a lot more than I know now."

"You really don't believe you know me?"

He shook his head at her. "I know some very important things."

"Such as?"

"That I love you."

"Ah, but you've only really known me a few months."

"A few days would have been sufficient."

"No. You don't mean that. When we, uh, got together, I wasn't even me. You fell for Holly."

"Okay. This has come up once before, and I'm going to put a stop to it right now."

"What?"

"Listen carefully. I love *you*. As Jane. You were never anyone else, not even for a moment. And what you did to me..."

She grinned, loving this part. "What?"

"You're shameless, you know that?"

"Uh-huh."

He narrowed his eyes a moment, but then his grin got the better of him. "You turned my world upside down."

She'd heard the words before, and it was wonderful to hear them again. Better than any fantasy.

"You breathed the life back into me."

"You would have been a sorry mess if I hadn't come around, huh?"

"A sorry mess."

She sighed again. "I know."

"Hey. I did some things for you, too, didn't I?"

She settled her head on his chest. "You gave me my

true self, and more happiness than anyone deserves. You made me incredibly glad to be Jane."

"Damn, I'm good."

"Speaking of being good..."

"Now?"

She nodded. "The beach is completely deserted."

"But there's the whole sand issue."

"The sand issue is what makes it exciting." She got to her feet, then yanked on his arms to pull him up. "We can pretend I've been shipwrecked. And that you've been living in the jungle, more beast than man."

He rolled his eyes as he stood. "Jane..."

"It'll be fun!"

"All right. But only on one condition."

"What?"

He kissed her lips tenderly. "Tonight, you're you and I'm me. Got it?"

She threw her arms around his neck. "I love you, Charley Warren."

"Charley Warren? I'm the dread pirate Brownbeard, stranded on my own island paradise, until a fierce storm came up last night...."

Pamela Burford presents

The Wedding Ring

Four high school friends and a pact—
every girl gets her ideal mate by thirty or be
prepared for matchmaking! The rules are
simple. Give your "chosen" man three
months...and see what happens!

Love's Funny That Way
Temptation #812—on sale December 2000
It's no joke when Raven Muldoon falls in love with comedy
club owner Hunter—*brother* of her "intended."

I Do, But Here's the Catch
Temptation #816—on sale January 2001
Charli Ross is more than willing to give up her status as
last of a dying breed—the thirty-year-old virgin—to Grant.
But all *he* wants is marriage.

One Eager Bride To Go
Temptation #820—on sale February 2001
Sunny Bleecker is still waiting tables at Wafflemania when
Kirk comes home from California and wants to marry her.
It's as if all her dreams have finally come true—except...

Fiancé for Hire
Temptation #824—on sale March 2001
No way is Amanda Coppersmith going to let
The Wedding Ring rope her into marriage. But no matter
how clever she is, Nick is one step ahead of her...

"Pamela Burford creates the
memorable characters readers love!"
—*The Literary Times*

It's hot...and it's out of control.

BLAZE

**This winter is going to be *hot, hot, hot!*
Don't miss these bold, provocative,
ultra-sexy books!**

SEDUCED by Janelle Denison
December 2000

Lawyer Ryan Matthews wanted sexy Jessica Newman the
moment he saw her. And she seemed to want him, too, but
something was holding her back. So Ryan decides it's time
to launch a sensual assault. He *is* going to have Jessica in
his bed—and he isn't above tempting her with her own
forbidden fantasies to do it....

SIMPLY SENSUAL by Carly Phillips
January 2001

When P.I. Ben Callahan agrees to take the job of watching
over spoiled heiress Grace Montgomery, he figures it's easy
money. That is, until he discovers gorgeous Grace has a
reckless streak a mile wide and is a serious threat to his
libido—and his heart. Ben isn't worried about keeping
Grace safe. But can he protect her from his loving lies?

Don't miss this daring duo!

Tyler Brides

It happened one weekend...

Quinn and Molly Spencer are delighted to accept three bookings for their newly opened B&B, Breakfast Inn Bed, located in America's favorite hometown, Tyler, Wisconsin.

But Gina Santori is anything but thrilled to discover her best friend has tricked her into sharing a room with the man who broke her heart eight years ago....

And Delia Mayhew can hardly believe that she's gotten herself locked in the Breakfast Inn Bed basement with the sexiest man in America.

Then there's Rebecca Salter. She's turned up at the Inn in her wedding gown. Minus her groom.

Come home to Tyler for three delightful novellas by three of your favorite authors: Kristine Rolofson, Heather MacAllister and Jacqueline Diamond.

HARLEQUIN®
Makes any time special ™

Visit us at www.eHarlequin.com   PHTB

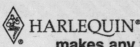

Harlequin proudly brings you

STELLA CAMERON
Bobby Hutchinson
Sandra Marton

in

MARRIED
IN SPRING

*a brand-new anthology in which three couples
find that when spring arrives, romance soon
follows...along with an unexpected
walk down the aisle!*

February 2001

Available wherever Harlequin books are sold.

HARLEQUIN®
Makes any time special ™

Visit us at www.eHarlequin.com

PHMARRIED